DEEP, DARK AND DEAD

The charge against Shane Stafford was 'Assault Occasioning Actual Bodily Harm'. Stafford had attacked a gossip journalist called Gavin Legge. Legge had been engaged at one time to Shane's twin sister. In Shane's view Legge had not just let down his sister, but had subsequently hounded her to suicide. It was the custom of the hot-tempered Stafford clan to stick together. But reckless actions have unpredictable — and even more ominous — consequences.

D1390972

DONALD MACKENZIE

DEEP, DARK AND DEAD

Complete and Unabridged

LINFORD
Leicester

First published in Great Britain

First Linford Edition
published 1997

British Library CIP Data

MacKenzie, Donald, *1918*–
    Deep, dark and dead.—Large print ed.—
Linford mystery library
1. Detective and mystery stories
2. Large type books
I. Title
813.5′4 [F]

ISBN 0–7089–5111–2

Published by
F. A. Thorpe (Publishing) Ltd.
Anstey, Leicestershire

Set by Words & Graphics Ltd.
Anstey, Leicestershire
Printed and bound in Great Britain by
T. J. International Ltd., Padstow, Cornwall

This book is printed on acid-free paper

For Anne N. Barrett with affection and gratitude for her patience, encouragement and shrewd judgement over the years.

1

IT was the second day of Shane Stafford's trial, another leaden day with rain sluicing across the courtroom windows. Emma Stafford and I were sitting up front in the public benches. Patrick Joseph O'Callaghan had finally decided not to call us as defence witnesses. Knightsbridge Crown Courts are built inside the shell of an Edwardian mansion on Hans Crescent and have the reputation of being the most comfortable courts in the city. They are carpeted throughout, with padded benches and seats, a restroom and a library. It's warm there in winter and cool in summer. Though the cafeteria food is terrible there are pubs nearby and Harrods sandwich bar is only just around the corner.

There are fifteen public seats in

Court Number Five but Emma and I were the only people there. On our left was the judge's bench under a large shield bearing a golden lion and white unicorn. The man occupying it put me in mind of my grandfather. He had the same tetchy shift of the buttocks whenever he found a remark unclear or foolish, the same searing sarcasm that started as a whinny and finished as a bellow.

Below him sat his clerk, a forceful-looking character with a bandit's moustache and a strong Scottish accent. Next to him was the court-reporter, a girl in a porridge-coloured dress with a centre parting in hay-brown hair and an expression of near-belief in what she was transcribing. Her attitude had been particularly pointed the day before when evidence given had obliged her to record some very basic language.

The lawyers had argued for a couple of hours over the composition of the jury, ending up with only one woman, a matron with a mouth like a fox-trap.

She had on harlequin spectacles and reminded me of one of those cleaning ladies you see coming out of public buildings, the ones who always wear trousers and headscarves and board buses smoking Virginian cigarettes. The men were an undistinguished bunch, the sort of guys you'd see on a line outside a football stadium any Saturday afternoon.

The dock was at the extreme end of the courtroom, separated from the judge's rostrum by the intervening rows of benches for barristers and solicitors. I could just see the top of Shane's shaggy red head and the balding scalp of the jailer sitting next to him.

Gavin Legge's bulk filled the witness box on our left. It was early March but he was just back from Nassau and deeply tanned. He was wearing the blue flannel suit he had worn the day before with a black silk knitted tie. Hands clasped easily behind his back, he cocked his head attentively as he listened to the questions the

3

prosecuting counsel put to him.

According to what Patrick Joseph O'Callaghan said, the police were treating the case as open and shut. The charge against Shane was one of *Assault Occasioning Actual Bodily Harm* and they reckoned to have the evidence they needed to win. They'd put up a lanky junior counsel called Waitland against us, a horse-faced individual who looked very pleased with himself. Apart from a couple of traffic violations at home in Canada I'd never been in a court before but Waitland seemed to me to be highly suspect.

I was by no means sure however that Shane was going to stand up to cross-examination. His hotheadedness was notorious and the last thing he could afford to do was to lose his cool. O'Callaghan had been drumming this into him all the time he had been on bail. *Whatever happens in court don't lose your temper!*

Waitland let his gown slip from one

shoulder, a coquettish gesture I figured he'd noted in someone else.

"Now, Mr. Legge! Am I correct in saying that you have known the defendant for almost four years?"

"It would be about that, yes." Legge had the odd, faintly cockney accent of his South African upbringing.

"How would you describe your relationship during that time?"

Legge thought for a moment then allowed himself the narrowest widening of the lips. His teeth were very white against the tan.

"That's not easy to say. You see we saw a lot of one another at the beginning, then things changed. There was, you know, a coolness. We'd run into one another here and there but we'd rarely speak."

Waitland's nod was designed to make Legge's answer seem both cogent and reasonable.

"Exactly. But you were still civil to one another?"

"Let's put it this way," said Legge.

"We were no longer friends but we certainly weren't enemies. Not as far as I was concerned anyway."

Waitland rose on his toes. "Let me take you back to the early hours of January seventh of this year. You have told His Honour and the jury how on that date you visited a discothèque called *Pluto*'s in the company of friends and that the defendant attacked you with a chair. We have heard the medical evidence from Doctor Soares that your cheekbone was fractured in two places as a result of this attack."

Legge's frown regretted the memory. "Yes."

Waitland spaced his next question, dwelling on each word. "Can you think of anything that you did on that particular night that would have provoked this assault? Anything at all?"

Legge's shoulders rose and fell. "Frankly, no. But then I couldn't be expected to know what goes on inside Stafford's head, obviously. As far as I'm concerned I can think of nothing."

"You bloody liar!" Emma's aside was loud enough for the judge to turn his head towards us. The uniformed cop on the door craned forward menacingly. I could see where we could quite easily be thrown out of the courthouse.

Emma shoved her hand deep in the pocket of my mackinaw. She was wearing no make-up and with her small square face looked about eighteen instead of twenty-eight. After three years living with her I could read the signs and was aware of possible trouble. We'd already had hints of it that morning, coming into the building. The security man at the entrance had asked to see inside her bag. Ever since the bomb scares it was normal practice and she'd done it the day before. But something in his manner got up her nose. I don't know whether his suspicion stemmed from the way we were dressed. I was in jeans and sneakers and my mackinaw was ten years old. Emma's outfit was pretty sloppy for a courtroom appearance but the security man's manner was on the heavy side. His "May I help you, Miss?" had the ring of a demand to know her business.

She'd straightened him out in her starchiest accent, explaining that she had the misfortune to be attending the prosecution of her brother who was on trial for having performed a public duty.

I grabbed her fingers in my pocket and held them hard. Waitland folded like a piece of trelliswork and Shane's counsel came to his feet. Trelawney's plump purpling nose jutted out under thatched grey eyebrows and he played the stops of his voice like an organ.

"Let me get one thing clear in my mind, Mr. Legge. You were engaged to be married to the defendant's twin sister, were you not?"

"I was."

"How long did the engagement last?"

"Almost two years."

"And was it Miss Stafford who broke it off finally?"

8

"She did. That's right."

Trelawney sidled along the bench and filled a glass from the water carafe.

"Did that come as a complete surprise to you or had you been expecting something of the sort to happen?"

Legge stared down at the brown and yellow carpet before answering. "No I wasn't. Not at that particular time, anyway."

"Does that mean that you have difficulty in remembering?" Trelawney asked sarcastically.

Legge showed his good teeth again. "Memories do play tricks, Mr. Trelawney, and I'm under oath."

Shane was sitting up much straighter now and I could see the whole of his face. His eyes were on Legge, his gaze as direct as a laser beam.

Trelawney worked his way back along the bench moving crabwise. "Were you resentful that your engagement had been broken off?"

"Resentful?" Legge shook his head.

"Look, Mr. Trelawney, I'm thirty-eight years old and I've been around. It wasn't the first time that I'd been jilted. I was disappointed — a little sad, if you like, but certainly not resentful."

The judge's tone was tinder-dry. "I suppose this *is* leading us somewhere, Mr. Trelawney?"

The defence counsel explained himself. "I'm much obliged to Your Honour. With respect, both question and answer have a definite bearing on my client's conduct on the morning of January seventh."

"Very well." The accent was English instead of Canadian but the voice was still my grandfather's.

Trelawney continued. "I'd like you if you would, Mr. Legge, to tell His Honour and members of the jury exactly what your feelings were for Miss Stafford. I mean subsequent to her breaking off the engagement."

Emma wriggled beside me. Her hair is the same colour as Shane's and flames like a fox's brush.

"I suppose you could say that I was emotionally disturbed," Legge admitted after a while. "You know, upset. You don't fall out of love overnight."

"Yerss," commented Trelawney, diminuendo. He went on with undisguised incredulity. "I understand that you are known professionally as 'The Voice They Cannot Silence'? Is this correct?"

Legge was a veteran of some thirty-odd libel suits and not about to be knocked offstride by sarcasm.

"That's correct, yes." If you didn't know Legge, the show of good-natured embarrassment would have been convincing.

Trelawney read from the paper in front of him. "A Chronicler Of Human Frailty?"

"That too." Legge squared his shoulders. "What I really am, Mr. Trelawney, is a working journalist reporting the events that make news."

"Gossip and scandal?"

"Events that make news," Legge insisted.

"Nothing is sacred to you, not even death?"

Waitland cranked himself up, his horseface indignant. The judge screwed his nose closer to his chin but Legge had already answered.

"As I understand it, sir, the word 'sacred' implies a belief in God. I have no religious beliefs." There was a ring of disarming honesty in the statement.

"How about pity, compassion? Do you believe in these, Mr. Legge? Would you say you're capable of feeling either?"

"As capable as you are, Mr. Trelawney." It was Legge's first mistake and the judge lost no time in letting him know it.

"The witness will confine himself to answering 'yes' or 'no'." He glanced across at the clock on the wall. It was ten past twelve. "The court will adjourn for fifteen minutes."

We all stood for his exit. The jury

retired to their room and Shane went back to the cells. Legge was already in the corridor chatting to the detective in charge of the case. A woman usher was smoking and the opposing counsel were exchanging banter.

I'd always had the impression that the British treat the matter of trying a man for his life or liberty with dignity and respect. Everything seems to encourage the concept, the formal stylized language and customs, the archaic wigs and gowns. I wasn't prepared for the total collapse of decorum the moment the judge disappeared, the complete indifference to the accused man.

I took Emma outside for a smoke. Legge and the detective moved out of earshot ostentatiously. Emma's hand worked nervously.

"What is Trelawney waiting for? Why doesn't he ask Legge about all those articles he wrote about Sara?"

"He will," I promised.

The prosecution had six witnesses.

The manager of *Pluto*'s, a couple of waiters, the detective who had made the arrest, Legge himself and the doctor who had treated his injuries at St. George's Hospital. We had spent the previous evening going over the case with O'Callaghan. In his opinion the only defence would be that of extreme provocation.

"You've got ash on your nose," I said to Emma. By the time she had finished with her hand mirror people were filing back into court. Trelawney came to his feet, a sheaf of press clippings in front of him, slow-timing his movements and adjusting his spectacles. I could tell that Legge knew exactly what was coming.

"What I propose to do," Trelawney announced, "is to read extracts that have been taken from your gossip columns over the period of the last two years. The first is dated June eleventh, roughly nine weeks after Miss Stafford broke off her engagement to marry you. I quote.

Friends tell me that the delectable Sara Stafford is to be seen leaving an address in Kinnerton Street in the early hours of the morning. The lovely Sara (twin brother Shane, ex-amateur jockey who runs a Chelsea estate agency) is Impressionist expert at the Oakley Gallery. Serge Blauberg the proprietor of the Oakley Gallery lives in Kinnerton Street. Watch this space for further news . . . "

Trelawney glanced over the top of his spectacles, at the judge first and then at the jury. He let the piece of paper fall from his fingers and picked up the next.

"This one is dated August twentieth of last year and printed under the heading

RED FACES AT THE OAKLEY GALLERY My legal spies inform me that a certain sheik from Kuwait has been advised to bring court action following the discovery that the

'Renoir' he purchased from the Oakley was painted on the island of Ibiza in 1964. Impressionist 'expert' Sara Stafford is believed to have found the 'Renoir' privately for her friend and principal Serge Blauberg. Miss Stafford is currently on holiday in Tobago and not available for comment."

Trelawney drank some more water, his nose appearing to have turned still a deeper shade of purple. He read on through a succession of clippings, some twenty of them, his musical voice lingering on the slurs and innuendos, emphasizing the double meanings. By the time he had come to the final piece of paper I could feel Emma's body shaking.

Trelawney's raised hand demanded attention. "November seventh, last year!

MR. MIDNIGHT LOSES A FRIEND
Habitués of Pluto's, Tramp and Annabel's were hardly surprised to

hear of Sara Stafford's departure from the London scene. Since losing her job at the Oakley Gallery, the erratic Miss Stafford, 33, has shown increasing signs of becoming tired and overemotional. I am able to reveal that the one time toast of Jermyn Street is presently resting in Forest Hill, an establishment in Surrey popular with those suffering from 'nervous disorders'. We wish Sara a speedy return to those who appreciate her very special talents."

Trelawney pushed the clippings along the bench with an air of contempt. Waitland gave them to the usher and they went from the judge to jury and were entered as exhibits. Trelawney gathered his robe. He was supposed to be talking to Legge but his eyes were on the jury. There was a sincerity and earnestness about his voice that was impressive but I didn't see where it was taking him.

"Shortly after that last scurrilous

report in your newspaper, Mr. Legge, Sara Stafford took her own life. I'm suggesting to you that you took advantage of your professional position to pursue a vendetta against a girl who was unable to defend herself. I'm suggesting that morally at least you are responsible for her death!"

There was a buzz in the courtroom and Waitland was up, his face red and outraged.

"This is too much, Your Honour! I really must protest!"

"Mr. Trelawney?" The judge's tone sounded mild enough to me.

Trelawney stood his ground. "With respect, Your Honour, I believe myself to be within rules. My duty is to put my client's case and my cross-examination goes directly to the issue."

"Well I'm not going to allow it," said the judge. He fiddled with his pen for a moment. "Not in that form, anyway. The witness need not answer the last question."

"Thank you, Your Honour." Legge's

back shed an invisible weight but the damage had been done and everyone in the room knew it.

"If Your Honour pleases," said Trelawney. "Very well, Mr. Legge, I put it to you that you entered *Pluto*'s discothèque in the early hours of January seventh knowing full well that the defendant was there. Not only that, I put it to you that you knew that he had attended his twin sister's cremation service the previous afternoon."

"That's ridiculous," said Legge. "I'd no idea Stafford was in the place until I saw him coming at me with a chair. And how could I know that he'd been to his sister's cremation service?"

"Because someone who works for you happened to be present. Someone who bothered to copy the names of the people who had sent flowers."

Legge shook his head slowly. "I've no idea why you're taking this line, Mr. Trelawney. If anyone from my office was present at the crematorium it wasn't on my instructions. Nor was I told about it. This is the truth."

"No more questions," said Trelawney. He sat down, looking back at Patrick Joseph O'Callaghan, his expression one of disbelief.

Legge was certainly lying. Emma and I had been at the cremation service with Shane and we'd seen one of Legge's team taking the names on the cards that accompanied the flowers. It was unlikely that this would have been done without his knowledge. He was about to leave the witness-box when Waitland stopped him. The prosecuting counsel was obviously intent on doing a repair job.

"In view of the allegations that have been made, perhaps you will explain to His Honour and members of the jury just how your articles are written. I'm referring in particular to the sources of your information and the policy you adopt in dealing with it.

"Who actually does the writing?"

Nothing could have suited Legge

better. I'd watched him on a couple of television talk shows, defending his function with arrogant confidence. He took his hands from behind his back and used them to emphasize his points.

"The main thing to remember is this — there's no distinction between public and private lives in our business."

The judge removed an invisible thread from his lavender front. His sash was scarlet and I noticed for the first time that his wig was different to the ones that counsel wore, with a tail but no side curls. He leaned sideways in the direction of Legge and his tone sharpened abruptly. There was something in his manner that put me in mind of a tailor inspecting a garment that he hasn't made.

"I'm sorry, Mr. Legge. Possibly I didn't understand you clearly. Are you saying that as far as you are concerned a person in public life has no right to privacy?"

Legge rode the judge's outrage as a gull does stormy water. "For a

21

journalist, no, Your Honour. We have our rules of behaviour certainly, set by the Press Council but within the framework of these rules you could say it's a free-for-all."

The judge contented himself with a tightmouthed smile but I had the feeling that Legge had struck out again. He continued.

"Without people feeding me information a column like mine couldn't exist. Investigatory journalism is time-consuming and whatever I print has to be topical. I've built up the best sources of information in the business and we budget for this. People call in for all sorts of reasons, people on the make, people with a score to settle. It would surprise you to know just who does contribute to my diary."

I sneaked a look at the foreman of the jury. He was listening to Legge with arms folded across his chest.

"And the column is published under your name?"

"I have three collaborators. Some of

the stories I handle myself, the big ones. And I edit what the others write. As you say, the column is published under my name and the final responsibility is mine."

"Exactly." Waitland gathered his papers. "I'd like to get one thing clear. Have you ever singled out any person or persons as the subject of your comments?"

Legge's smile flared. "Absolutely not, sir. They do that themselves. It's a question of lifestyle. I've heard it said that you can't con a man who doesn't have larceny in his heart. It's something like that in our business. We're reporters, not character assassins. We can't expose what isn't there."

The judge glanced up from his notes, looking at the clock. Waitland's manner was confidential.

"A lot has been made of the fact that Miss Stafford's name appears in a number of articles from your column over the past two years. Is this abnormal?"

Legge shook his head. "There are people who are in my columns every week. I told you, it's a question of life styles. Let me get something straight for the record. Not one of those pieces about Sara Stafford was written by me. I left them in because in my opinion they were news and Sara Stafford had no special claim to exemption. I'm sorry to have to say this but over the period we're dealing with everything this girl did or touched seemed to go sour. If we hadn't printed the stories about her others would. It's as simple as that."

"Did you," and now the words came very deliberately, "at any time have the intention of hounding this unfortunate girl to her death?"

Legge looked the length of the court to where Shane was sitting. "How *could* this have been possible? Whatever happened between us we had once been in love. If it hadn't been for her family things wouldn't have turned out as they did."

"Thank you, Mr. Legge. That concludes the case for the prosecution, Your Honour."

Waitland resumed his seat and Legge took a place in the row behind us. I could feel Emma start to shake again. The judge collected his papers, smiling over at the jury.

"I'm sure you're all hungry, members of the jury, and this seems a convenient time to adjourn. The court will resume at two o'clock."

He bobbed his head and disappeared through a door. Shane had been on bail for almost three months but for some reason they now kept him in custody. Emma, O'Callaghan and I walked west to Walton Street and a pub on the corner. We were ten minutes ahead of the lunchtime rush and we found a free corner table. There was curried beef on the menu and we drank Guinness.

I found myself thinking that if ever I were up on a charge Patrick Joseph O'Callaghan would be my man. He's thirty-five years old, intelligent and literate and has an instinctive flair for the defence. He just wants his clients to win. As he puts it, he might not be sure that a man is innocent. But then it isn't his job to judge but to argue the case the best way he can. Patrick Joseph wears his hair long for a lawyer, doesn't get much sun on his skin and has those dark-blue Irish eyes. His Inverness cape and rosebud have given him a reputation for eccentricity but underneath the theatrical flamboyancy there's an assurance that goes with having it made at the age of thirty-five. Success allows him to take only the cases that interest him. If he hadn't been a personal friend of the Staffords I don't think he'd have touched Shane's brief with a bargepole.

Emma shoved her plate to one side and lighted a cigarette. She'd eaten practically nothing and her glass was still half-empty.

"How do you think it's going, Patrick Joseph?" Her voice was casual but I knew her too well to suppose it was anything but a cover up.

He raised a shoulder without saying anything in reply. I bought myself another Guinness. O'Callaghan was removing shreds of curried beef with a small gold toothpick.

"I wouldn't have thought that Legge did too well," I ventured. "I'm sure Shane will come out better."

"He's not being called." O'Callaghan put his toothpick away. "Trelawney decided against it."

Emma scraped her chair back, her eyes bulging. "You mean you're going to let that creep get away with telling all those lies and not give Shane a chance to tell his side of the story?"

O'Callaghan waved her down, grinning. "Let's not have any of your dramatics, Emma. The thing is, the judge is sympathetic at the moment. That much is obvious. If we put Shane in the box and Waitland gets to him we risk losing that sympathy."

"What the hell has the judge to do with it?" Emma demanded. She lowered her voice in response to O'Callaghan's warning look. Legge and the cop were only feet away, standing at the bar. "How about the jury?"

O'Callaghan leaned across the table. "You might as well make your minds up to this, both of you. Shane's chance of being acquitted is about one in a hundred. *That*'s why we need to keep the judge on our side. He's going to do the sentencing."

"You mean that my brother can actually go to jail?" She made it sound like imminent crucifixion.

O'Callaghan nodded. "He'll be lucky if he doesn't."

She looked at me for reassurance but I couldn't give her any. I guess I'd always suspected the truth since the cops called us in the middle of the night to say that they had Shane in the cells. I'd attended court the following day and had been one of Shane's sureties for bail. I couldn't get much out of him those first few hours and Legge was still in hospital under observation. All Shane would say was that Legge had insulted Sara and struck the first blow. The waiters and the manager of *Pluto*'s all claimed that the aggressor was Shane, but he was almost my brother-in-law.

O'Callaghan turned his wrist. "It's a quarter to two. We'd better be getting back."

The same security man was on duty at the courthouse entrance. Emma dumped the contents of her purse on the table in front of him, her glare daring him to make some sort of comment. This time there was none. The judge followed the jurors into court and Trelawney came to his feet.

"The defence calls no witnesses, Your Honour."

A couple of the jurors sneaked a look at Shane and I had a rough idea what they must be thinking. An innocent man goes into the box and tells his side of the story. Shane's freckle-blotched face was pale under the overhead strip lighting. It seemed to me now that the British way of producing a man accused of a crime was unfair. There's supposed to be this assumption of innocence until proven guilty yet the defendant is cut off from the main body of people, boxed and guarded like a felon.

Waitland kept his closing speech short. "Members of the jury, His Honour will instruct you in the matter of your duty both to the defendant and that body of his peers that you have the privilege to represent. I haven't the slightest doubt that you will discharge your burden with discretion, arriving at your verdict according to evidence that you have heard in court. It is upon that evidence alone, members of the jury, that your verdict must be reached. The defendant is charged upon indictment of an Assault Occasioning Actual Bodily Harm, of striking one Simon Legge with a chair and fracturing his left cheekbone in two places. The facts in this case are clear and unchallenged. The accused *did* assault Mr. Legge with a chair. Mr. Legge's cheekbone *was* fractured. My learned friend has suggested that his client's action was in self-defence but he produced no evidence at all to bolster this suggestion. No, members of the jury, the only verdict open to you is one of Guilty. I invite you to return it with confidence."

Emma grabbed my hand under the skirt of my mackinaw. Trelawney spoke longer. He seemed to me to be working under pressure, like a conjuror at a party of blasé children. He struggled on, producing rabbits here, fluttering doves and cards from his sleeves but one felt that it was all an illusion. *I* felt. And my guess was that this was the jury's feeling. The defendant, he said, was part of what was clearly a close-knit family. The strong emotional bond between twins was a phenomenon well-known to psychologists. Simon Legge had made use of his newspaper columns to pursue a girl mercilessly over a period of two years. "And what of the events of seventh January? A young man has just seen his dead sister's body committed to the furnaces of a crematorium. The memory is too sharp and bitter to carry back to a lonely flat. He takes it to a place where the dead girl and he had spent many happy hours. And what happens to him there? He is confronted by Mr. Legge who first insults and then strikes him. A scuffle ensues. Now, members of the jury, you have seen Mr. Legge. He's a big man, physically at least, twice the size of the defendant. It isn't too difficult to put yourself in Mr. Stafford's place at that moment. Here he is, bereaved and wanting only to be alone with his memories and hears his dead sister insulted. What would any of you do in such a position, members of the jury? You'd object, of course and with anyone else but Mr. Legge you'd attempt to remonstrate. But he is not only berated, he is physically assaulted. In fear, he picks up a chair to defend himself. Now self-defence is a legitimate and logical form of behaviour. The laws of our land accept this. And this is what my client's behaviour was, members of the jury, legitimate self-defence. His actions need no further justification and I ask you to acquit him."

There was an outbreak of coughing and shuffling of feet. Trelawney's speech had been florid and from where I sat pretty unconvincing. The judge began his summing up. Once again it was my grandfather, speaking in front of the drawing room fire, unmoved by tears or emotional pleas, dispassionately establishing the facts. Except in this case he reminded the jury of the evidence they had heard, advising them of the legal interpretation and telling them that they alone were judges of fact.

The jury retired and they took Shane away to the cells again. Emma and I stayed in our seats, close together but silent. My own mind was busy with other matters, for instance what was going to happen if they sent Shane to jail. I run a kind of theatrical agency that specializes in producing stunt-men for television and film work. If somebody needs a man to jump a horse, freefall from an aeroplane or take a roundhouse swing to the jaw, we furnish the athlete. Work is on and off and there's usually plenty of spare time. I'm thirty-six years old, five feet eleven and no more than a couple of pounds overweight for my age and height. I walk a lot and manage to get in a day a week with the Surrey Farmers Hunt during the season. A lot of the jobs that come through the office I handle myself. Otherwise I help Emma with the office chores. We work out of our mews house. There's enough to do to make me wonder how I'd be able to handle Shane's business as well as my own. He runs a small but specialized estate agency. There's a pretty girl who acts as his receptionist and secretary and sleeps with him whenever they both fancy it. The agency depends entirely on Shane's charm and drive and I could see no way of replacing him even temporarily.

It seemed a long time to me and in fact the jury was back in two and a half hours, unable to arrive at a verdict. The judge didn't appear to hear the news any too happily. He shifted in his seat, picking at the end of his nose reflectively. He mumbled something about the waste of time and public money then cleared his throat and buttered up the jurors with a tribute to their patience.

"I can now accept a majority verdict of at least ten of you whatever it be, 'guilty' or 'not guilty'. Having said that I shall say no more. Will you now please retire again and consider your verdict."

I could feel the warmth of Emma's thigh against mine and sense her anxiety. Spiritually she was standing in the dock with her brother and would have torn Legge apart given the chance. The jurors filed out and I wondered which of them if any was on our side.

To get to their room they had to pass close to the dock. None as much as glanced sideways. They all kept their heads averted as though embarrassed by the knowledge that Shane's liberty was in their hands.

Emma and I joined the crowd in the main lobby. There were only two benches and people stood in groups linked awkwardly by circumstances. Defendants, their families and friends, cops in and out of uniform, the plainclothes men distinguished by the fact that their eyes were never still.

The smell of the wet street drifted in every time the glass entrance doors were opened. Nobody smiled and the general air of depression was beginning to get to me.

"What are you thinking about?" Emma asked suddenly. The way she puts this question, out-of-context and unexpectedly, still takes me by surprise. It isn't that she really wants to know. It's a reminder that she's there.

She has a blotch of freckles across

the bridge of her nose and her eyes are grey-green. She uses them like a searchlight. I've learned a lot about loving from her. The best way to shut her up is to kiss her. I did this under the frosty stare of the security man at the entrance. There was a noise over the p.a. system, like somebody clearing his throat and then a voice.

"Will counsel concerned in the case of Stafford please go at once to Court Number Five."

I grabbed Emma by the arm. "Come on, that's us. The jury's back."

We slid into our seats as the judge rustled in. The jurors were already back in their places, Legge behind us. Shane was sitting bolt upright and raised a hand as he saw us. The clerk of the court rose and faced the jury.

"Have you reached a verdict, Mr. Foreman?"

"We have." He was tightmouthed and stood with his hands behind his back.

"Is it 'guilty' or 'not guilty'?"

The foreman blinked a couple of times. "Guilty."

Trelawney gathered the papers in front of him, his face a study in ostentatious disgust. The clerk droned on.

"And is that the verdict of all of you?"

"It is, yes."

Whoever had been on our side couldn't have held out very long. So much for the courage of their convictions. I glanced at Shane. His face had gone very red. I just managed to grab Emma as she started to rise. Her bottom hit the seat with a thud. The detective in charge of the case took the stand and read what he called Shane's 'antecedents'.

"The defendant is thirty-three years old, single and lives at number one hundred and fifty-five, Lennox Gardens, S.W.1, Your Honour. He is a director of an estate agency with offices at the same address. He was educated at Eton College and in Switzerland,

Your Honour, and he has no criminal history."

Shane was up and standing at attention, his hands pressing against the seams of his trousers like a drill-sergeant. I'd known him since I'd taken up with Emma and everything that Trelawney had said was correct. The Staffords *were* a closely-knit family and the bond between Emma and Shane had been even tighter since Sara's suicide. I liked him without professing to understand him. But then I don't understand Emma either. There's a no-go area in their make-up in which they prowl around, growling softly and lashing their tails. It isn't a place for a stranger.

It was at this moment that Trelawney displayed a card nobody knew about except O'Callaghan obviously. He rose to his feet.

"With Your Honour's permission I would like to call evidence of character."

The judge frowned, scratching the

back of his head beneath the wig.

"That isn't necessary, surely? His character has never been at issue and his antecedents are blameless enough."

Trelawney stood his ground. "With respect, Your Honour, I would like the Court to hear this witness."

The judge's tone was testy. "You know as well as I do, Mr. Trelawney, that this isn't a case for this kind of procedure. It's a sheer waste of time."

"Again with respect, Your Honour." Trelawney showed no sign of being cowed. "I'm suggesting that its precisely because of the nature of this case that the Court should hear someone who has known my client since he was a child."

Shane's face had gone brick-red again. The judge seemed to read something there that decided him.

"Very well, you may call your witness, subject to the usual rules of evidence."

Emma must have guessed what Trelawney was up to. Her grip tightened on my arm as the corridor door opened. A bailiff ushered in a tiny woman dressed in decent black and wearing a basin-shaped hat. She must have been close to eighty but her voice was perfectly clear. It was an old-fashioned voice and belonged to an age when a servant was part of the family.

Trelawney spoke courteously. "Is your name Hilda Bailey and do you live at number twenty-three Parsons Green Close, S.W.6?"

She took one quick look at Shane and then turned away, refusing the judge's invitation to sit down.

"That's right. Miss Hilda Bailey."

"And are you a retired children's nurse?"

She nodded quickly. "Nanny Bailey, sir. I was Nanny Bailey for fifty years, twenty-five of them with the same family."

"That would be with the Staffords?"

"The Staffords, yes. Then when the accident happened, Mr. Wells — he was one of the trustees — he asked me

41

to stay on and look after the children. There were no other relations. I never thought of myself as a housekeeper. I was still Nanny to the children. The twins were eleven and Miss Emma no more than six."

"Tell us about this accident, Nanny Bailey."

She shut her eyes for a moment, using her memory. "It was just after teatime, a lovely spring day. The children were home from school and we were all out in the garden. Both the twins and Miss Emma were going to a day-school nearby. Mr. and Mrs. Stafford didn't like them separated. It was that kind of family, sir. We lived in Suffolk, the Old Malt House."

The mixture of sadness and sincerity was holding everyone's attention. Shane's eyes never left her as though sure that somehow she could save him. I could hear Emma's breathing, hurried and anxious.

Nanny Bailey continued. "Mr. and Mrs. Stafford had gone into Bury St.

Edmunds in the car. I heard the ringing in the house. It was the police on the telephone. Mr. and Mrs. Stafford had been run into by a brewer's lorry. They were killed on the spot, both of them. I stayed in the library, wondering how I was going to tell the children. I can remember praying and God gave me the courage to go outside to them. Only the little one cried. The twins seemed to be struck dumb. Master Shane's face had gone as white as a sheet. I shall never forget what he said to his sisters. 'We're alone now,' he said. 'Forever and ever. So we must make a pact not to desert one another'. And they never did, sir, not until . . . "

Trelawney's face was sympathetic as she used the scrap of linen. Even then she was unable to finish the sentence.

"Not till Miss Sara . . . "

I'd never been able to determine whether the Staffords' abnormal aggressive clannishness stemmed from the violent death of their parents. The answer seemed to be somewhere there in the gentle memory of this old lady. What she could never have supplied was the answer to Legge's lure for Sara. I guessed that the totally unscrupulous must have held some kind of fascination for her.

The judge glanced across at the clock on the wall. Trelawney didn't move physically but seemed to float nearer his witness.

"When the children finally went to their boarding-schools, you stayed on in the house, keeping it as a home for them. They would spend their holidays there?"

She nodded firmly. "It *was* their home, sir."

Trelawney's voice was direct. "I want you to tell His Honour in your own words the sort of man Shane Stafford is."

The answer came spontaneously. "He's kind, generous and honest, sir. A gentleman who's never let down a friend. I just don't understand seeing him where he is today." For the second time she was close to tears.

Trelawney let her go and Waitland had no questions. Nanny Bailey left the stand and took a seat on the other side of Emma.

The judge donned his spectacles. God knows why since he wasn't reading. Maybe it was a prop that he needed when sentencing. His tone was completely unemotional.

"Shane Stafford, you are an extremely fortunate young man. You have been found guilty — and quite rightly so in my opinion — of a violent assault that might well have ended with far more serious consequences. I've listened carefully to everything that has been said on your behalf by learned counsel and others and I accept the fact that your sister suffered a series of offensive attacks in a national newspaper. Furthermore I'm prepared to accept that these attacks might well have affected the balance of this unfortunate young lady's mind. Nevertheless, the protection of the law embraces everyone, including the writers of gossip-columns. I sentence you to twelve months' imprisonment to be suspended for two years.

"This means that you are free to leave now. Keep out of trouble for two years and you'll hear nothing more of this affair. On the other hand, if you find yourself in court during that period you will serve the twelve months' sentence in addition to any other punishment that might be imposed."

The court broke up. The foreman of the jury was looking relieved as if he agreed with the judge's clemency. Shane came through the door in the dock and Nanny Bailey and Emma hurried to meet him.

There were papers for him to sign and he went off with O'Callaghan. The old lady was badly distressed and I waited as Emma put her in a cab. Shane came back wearing the first real smile I had seen on his face in weeks. He has a strange mixture of attitudes that at least have the merit of being unstudied. The way he had dressed for his courtroom appearance was somehow representative of them. He was wearing a dark blue flannel suit with little cuffs on the sleeves but no tie. It's the same with so many things. He detests rock-and-roll music but spends a fair amount of time in discothèques. He needs the company of women yet offers them little in return.

I gave him my hand. "Well done that man!"

He shoved his fingers through his red hair, revealing the livid scar on his forehead, souvenir of a fall at Cheltenham. It's a hard way to land, from the back of a horse travelling at thirty-five miles an hour.

"It's over," he said shortly. "That's all that matters. Let's get the hell out of here."

We went past the security men and down the steps to the street. It was still raining. My car was parked just around the corner on Pavilion Road and while

Shane walked with me, Emma and Patrick Joseph O'Callaghan hurried on ahead. Suddenly Legge appeared from nowhere, large, bronzed and grinning. He stuck his hand out at Shane as he neared us. There was a photographer just behind us, a guy in a Scott Fitzgerald cap and with a press-camera. Shane moved back instinctively, trying to snatch his hand away but Legge was quicker and managed to make contact. He pumped Shane's arm, continuing to grin as the camera clicked a few feet away. Only Shane and I were able to hear what he was saying.

"You're a tramp like your sister, Stafford, and I'm going to give you the same treatment. That's a promise!"

He dropped Shane's hand but stood there still smiling. I stepped in between them quickly.

"Fuck off before I break your head," I said savagely.

A car cruised up and Legge and the photographer clambered in. A group of people had gathered on the pavement and stood watching curiously from under their umbrellas. I pushed Shane on and kept him moving till we reached the car. Emma took one look at Shane's face and snapped, "What's the matter?"

I shrugged. Anger flared in her face. "Is someone going to tell me what happened or not?"

I explained. Patrick Joseph O'Callaghan flapped the skirt of his cape. "That one's not hard to explain. Legge had set it up. The photographer was waiting. You can read the headlines. *Gossip Columnist Criticized By Judge Offers Hand of Friendship To Attacker*.

Emma's eyes were furious. "You mean nobody else heard what Legge said to Shane? How is that possible? There were people there, the photographer!"

I shook my head. "He kept his voice down and the photographer was a good fifteen feet away."

The gutter over Shane's head was spouting water but he didn't appear to notice it. He was staring up Pavilion Road in the direction taken by Legge's car. O'Callaghan checked his watch. "I have to get back to my office. I wouldn't worry about Legge. He's done his worst."

Emma has her own set of car-keys and was opening the door on her side. She swung round suddenly, glaring at O'Callaghan.

"'Done his worst'? What the hell is that supposed to mean?"

He's a gentle person by nature but I could tell that he was losing his patience.

"In the car," I told her.

She stood her ground, still facing O'Callaghan. "I'll get in when I'm good and ready. I'm asking Patrick Joseph what we're supposed to do about Legge."

"Nothing," he said quietly.

I live with her loyalty. It's fierce, demanding and unshakeable. But sometimes it's hard to take, especially for someone who isn't as involved with her as I am. I tried to soft-pedal the issue.

"What Patrick Joseph's saying is that Legge *wanted* Shane to take a swing at him, recorded then and there on film. It would have been perfect, right outside the court where he had just had his sentence suspended. This time he *would* have gone to jail. But Legge blew it. Now hop in and we'll all go home."

I drive an old XK 120 convertible with two proper seats and a couple of places for dwarfs in back. Shane wedged himself in behind and I took the wheel. Patrick took the rosebud from his cloak and reached across in front of me to give it to Emma.

"Trust Patrick Joseph. It's over, Emma. Legge's been discredited in open court and it's going to take him some time to live that down. Stay away from him, avoid the places where you're likely to meet him. At least for a while. Ok?"

She looked at the rosebud doubtfully. "Ok," she said quietly.

He walked away and we sat there

in silence, Emma staring beyond the flicking windshield wipers, Shane huddled behind. I put my palm against her cheek gently.

"I accept your apology."

This time she laughed. "You're a monster, Hamilton, and I don't know why I love you."

"Because I'm lovable." I twisted my neck addressing Shane. "You want to come back with us? Stay for dinner and play some Zilch?"

He considered it briefly but decided against. "I've got to do some thinking. You can drop me off at Lennox Gardens."

I was on the point of saying something when Emma's foot landed hard above my ankle. I moved the car round the corner to Shane's place. He works out of a three-storey white fronted house. The lower part he uses as an office and lives above. The basement is crammed with paintings and furniture that came from their parents' home in Wiltshire. A lot of it is valuable. For instance he's got a Turner in a broom cupboard along with a couple of French bronzes and a Queen Anne fourposter in pieces. He won't part with as much as a spoon and Emma encourages him. They're both like that, hoarders of artifacts and past memories. I opened the car door and let him out. He ran up the steps without looking back and the street door slammed.

It was four o'clock in the afternoon and the rest of the day promised nothing. I lighted a cigarette.

"What was all the kicking on the ankle about?"

She wound down her window. Whenever she's not smoking herself she's fastidious about the smell of my *Celtiques*.

"I just wanted you to leave Shane alone. Not fuss. He's better on his own at the moment."

It was good news if true. I have a lot of time but we had been holding his hand for what seemed an eternity.

"Great," I said heartily. She was in

53

a strange kind of mood and I walked warily. "So what do you have in mind for us?"

She didn't appear to hear me. "I've got to think, Jamie." It appeared to be catching. Shane had said exactly the same thing.

Nevertheless I bought it. "Think about what?"

She shook her head, leaning forward with her head hanging down and pushing the red hair up from her neck. Damp tendrils of a darker red clung to the nape of her neck. It was at times like this that I felt closest to her. She looked so vulnerable. She swung her head sideways suddenly.

"What *can* he do to Shane, Jamie?"

"You mean Legge?" I raised a shoulder. "Not too much I guess. Patrick Joseph's probably right. That performance outside the courthouse was Legge's last stand."

Her voice was unconvinced. "I don't believe it. You told me he said he'd do the same to Shane as he did to Sara."

"That's bullshit," I retorted. "He's just running his mouth." I pitched my cigarette-butt into the street. Her death-doom-and-disaster moods always exasperate me. The motor roared under my foot.

The lights were on up in Shane's apartment. I could see Amanda in the office downstairs, using the phone. With any sort of luck they would help one another over the next few hours. For my money what Shane needed now was a bottle of scotch and a woman, the chance to unwind.

I drove Emma home to Stanhope Mews, put the car away and followed her up the stairs. We have a tiny house, one bedroom, a sitting room, kitchen and bath over a one-car garage. It's a quiet central location and there's an enormous ginger cat living in the mews that has cleared the area of pigeons. Emma was lying on the sofa with her legs up and her eyes closed. I pay the rent but all the furniture is hers. The maple bed and commodes, the satin-upholstered sofa had been her mother's. The desk and hunting-prints had come from her father's study. The Staffords had lost their money in one of Rosenberg's mutual fund operations and conveniently killed themselves in a car accident the following spring. 'Conveniently' is Emma's choice of adverb. Her father had never done a stroke of work in his life and her mother adored him. Better, claimed Emma, that they went together and quickly. It may sound like pretty tough thinking from a girl of her age but her attitude to death is unconventional.

Sara Stafford had killed herself on a Saturday. The next day Emma called her. She tried again during the afternoon and that evening I drove her over to Sara's apartment. Neither of us had a key but I finally broke a window. We found Sara dead, her wrists slashed with a razor blade, her hair floating in a bath full of bloodied water. Emma called Shane and the police in that order, completely calm after that first look of horror and shock. She'd even tidied the flat while we waited, done the washing-up. I knew how much the loss of her sister meant to her. They'd been three and now they were two. She wept, her grief lasting through the night then never shed another tear, at least not for Sara.

I drew the velvet curtains, shutting out the misery of the wet cobblestones and got the fire going. One of the advantages of living in what had once been a coachman's dwelling is that we have a coal fire and a chimney that never smokes. Emma opened her eyes as I switched on the pedestal-lamp.

"How many people do you say have sued Legge for libel?"

"The line forms on the right," I answered. "And he's won them all except a couple that his newspaper have settled out of court. The bastard's untouchable. He's got a charmed life."

I went into the kitchen and plugged the kettle in for tea. There were crumpets in the breadbin. Later on we tried to play some chess and Emma lost two quick games in succession without making as much as a token objection. It was a sure sign that her mind wasn't on the game. I put the pieces away and poured her a glass of wine. I knocked the cap off a bottle of Budweiser and we made a salad. A film chase was showing on television and I tried to pick holes in the action shots.

The phone rang about nine. Emma took the call on the bedroom extension. The door was half-closed and I couldn't hear what she was saying but she was on the line for half-an-hour. She came back, refilled her glass and sat staring into the fire, chewing her upper lip. When she screws up her eyes it alters the whole shape of her face, making her look like a redheaded Pekinese. Then she nodded to herself, without saying anything. It's an unconscious trick but one that never fails to irritate me. Rain was coming down the chimney and I put more coal on the spitting fire.

"Was that Shane?"

She shook herself out of her reverie. "Yes."

"Is Amanda with him?"

"No, she's not." For someone who lives with a guy who isn't her husband, Emma can be strangely disapproving of other people's sexual mores.

"A pity," I said. "I'd have thought it's just the time he needed her. What's on his mind?"

She switched off the television and sat at my feet in front of the fire on the bearskin.

"I'm worried about him, Jamie."

The third Budweiser didn't have the fresh bite of the first. "Of course you're worried about him. *Everybody*'s worried about him. Maybe he'd be better off if they weren't."

"I'll remind you of that when you need a friend," she snapped, biting off the words as if they were my fingers.

I raised a hand in defeat. "Ok. I'll worry about him. What is it this time?"

Her head was between my knees, her

arms around my legs. "Legge called him a couple of hours ago. He said he's going to make it impossible for Shane to do business."

"Let's stop with the bullshit," I said. "There's no way that Legge can do that and we know it."

She closed a hole in her sock with her thumb and forefinger. Her voice had gone very quiet.

"He killed my sister, didn't he?"

It was after ten. I did the washing-up. We have no set rules for living. Whoever happens to be around and feels like it takes care of the household chores and the cooking. Emma was still sitting in front of the fire when I returned to the living room. Her head was hanging down, her hair screening her face.

I kissed the back of her neck, wishing that I could do something to pull her out of her downer. Our relationship is a good one, close enough for us to be able to touch without smothering. She twisted her head, looking up at me, very near to the tears she so despises.

"I hate him, Jamie! Why should he be able to do this to us?"

I didn't like seeing her this way but bums like Legge were facts of life like roaches in pizza parlours. Short of catching him in an alleyway one night I couldn't see what could be done about him.

I put my arms around her and lifted her to her feet. "Bed," I said.

We lay in the darkness, our bare bodies fitted together like spoons, listening to the patter of rain on the slates overhead, the occasional wet whisper of a car crossing the cobblestones. Her breast heaved under my cupped hand and I knew that she was sobbing. I'd no idea why. It could have been for Shane or for Sara — even for me. All I could do was tighten my hold on her and silently promise to love and protect her. Written down these are words that I'd normally shy at yet there's nothing to take their place.

I woke first as usual. It was twenty

past seven. The storage heaters had kept the flat warm though the fire had died. I made tea, boiled a couple of eggs and collected the mail and newspapers from the mat inside the front door. I carried the tray into the bedroom and took my place beside Emma. She's a slow, sleepy waker but a goodnatured one. She smiled contentedly, pulling the sheets up over her naked breasts. The misery of the night before appeared to be forgotten. I gave her the mail. She started flipping through it, her smile changing to a yawn. The rain had stopped, offering a glimpse of March grey skies through the window. I drank my tea, opened the *Globe* and turned to Legge's column.

The picture facing me was quarter-page size, shot from an angle and showed Legge, bronzed and smiling, extending the hand of forgiveness and friendship. The photographer had caught Shane and me glowering like a couple of heavies in a bad movie. The caption read:

ALL'S WELL THAT ENDS WELL

The so-called feud between Shane Stafford (for it is he) and your reporter ended yesterday outside Knightsbridge Crown Courts. A lenient judge having previously suspended Shane's prison sentence of a year for his attack on me, the combative little estate agent was overcome by remorse and offered me his apologies. Never one to hold a grudge I was glad to accept. The kindly old judge had warned Shane about his future conduct but spies tell me this was unnecessary. Shane is resolved to be ON HIS BEST BEHAVIOUR.

I put the paper down and closed my eyes. It was too late to hide the piece. I heard the bed creak as Emma reached across. I expected some sort of explosion but her voice was quite controlled.

"That really is it. Something just has to be done about this man."

I carried the breakfast tray to the kitchen and left the things for Mrs Patton to deal with. She gives us two hours of her day, five days a week. She deals with the fire, the stairs and the laundry. Emma was running her bath when the phone rang. I took it.

Shane's voice was shaking with anger. "What do you think of the bastard now!"

Emma took the phone from me. She had collected a towel from the bathroom and sat on the side of the bed, the towel draped around her body. The water was still running. I turned off the faucets and stepped into the tub. I had shaved, put on my jeans and sweater and gone through the mail by the time Emma finally hung up. The only thing of interest in the post was an inquiry from a television director looking for six acrobatic horsemen to use in a remake of *The Three Musketeers*.

I lowered the sitting room window and let fresh air into the flat. A hint of raw fog mingled with the smell of

Emma's *Calèche*. She was wearing a pair of tartan trews, a reefer jacket and had stuffed her hair into a green knitted cap. It was no more than a quarter to nine by the carriage clock on the mantelpiece and she never leaves the house before ten.

"Where are you going?" I demanded.

She picked up a scarf that matched her cap. "We're going round to Shane's. Both of us."

She'd used lipstick as well as scent and looked determined. I finished tying the laces of my sneakers.

"Am I allowed to know *why* we're going to Shane's."

"To talk," she said impatiently. She scribbled a note for Mrs. Patton and weighted it down with some money. The temperature outside had dropped ten degrees overnight. There was frost on the cobblestones and the mews cat was on his favourite perch, a window-ledge within sprinting distance of anything feathered that landed. The old XK 120 needs a warming-up period and it was another ten minutes before we were out of there. We cut across the park vying with the cowboys who seem to drive taxis these days and avoiding the shivering long-distance runners. A string of early morning riders reminded me that I'd be out with the Surrey Drag Hunt the following Saturday. It's one of the things I do alone. Emma doesn't ride.

It was early enough to find a parking meter almost outside Shane's house. He'd left the street door open for us. Amanda doesn't get in before ten. A watery sun was streaming in through the back window in the hallway, lighting the dark blue carpet and the paintings of eighteenth-century Staffords. I could smell coffee brewing upstairs. We climbed up to the mahogany door which was also open. The walls of Shane's living room are white and he has them hung with Bosch prints. The old sofa and armchairs sag in all the right places and were originally red. Shane knocked two windows into one when he bought the house, giving himself a fantastic view of the other side of the street. He seems to like it.

Emma went straight to the kitchen. Shane was over behind the sofa, feeding his goddam fish. Tiny wisps of colour darted through the rocks and greenery, goggled spellbound at the pipe that aerates the water. There's a Siamese fighting-fish that charges its own mirrored image.

"He's gone too far," Shane said quietly. He'd cut himself shaving and looked as though he had passed a rough night. But he was dapper in grey flannel trousers and a charcoal sweater. Emma appeared, carrying a tray with a coffeepot and cups. The Staffords do this kind of thing with one another, without previous discussion or invitation, as if they read each other's thoughts. It had been worse still with Sara and Shane.

Emma threw her cap and scarf on the sofa and poured the coffee. "Ok, we might as well get it out in the open. Something has to be done about Legge."

There's a picture of Sara on Shane's desk and the likeness between them is startling even for twins. It showed her on some kind of yacht, hair streaming in the wind and laughing. It was a happy picture. I wondered what the love of my life was about to lay on me.

"He simply has to be taught a lesson," she added.

The coffee was good. Shane wiped his mouth on the back of his hand.

"I had a call from a client at eight-thirty this morning. She wanted the keys of a house I'm trying to sell for her. She says she's changed her mind and is keeping it. That's balls. The truth is that she read that article this morning."

His glance at Emma was an unvoiced question that she answered immediately.

"I don't care who tells him."

I put my cup on the floor by my feet. "As long as somebody tells me, yes."

"We've decided to kidnap Legge," Emma announced.

My leg shot out involuntarily, my foot catching the coffee cup and spilling the contents across the light grey carpet.

"Abduct him," said Shane as if the change of verb somehow made it sound better.

Emma fetched a cloth from the kitchen and looked up from her kneeling position.

"What's the matter, Jamie? You're always complaining that nothing ever happens. Well here's your chance. Something *is* happening and you can be part of it."

I stared at the kidney shaped stain on the carpet. Emma was scrubbing at it in an aimless sort of way. I'd hoped that what she was saying was some kind of bad joke. The expression on her face told me that it wasn't.

"You're crazy," I said. "Irresponsible and downright dangerous."

Incredibly enough, she smiled. Shane

fixed me with his blue blaze. I've seen the same look on those people who come to the street door offering to put you in touch with God. What it generally means is that they have a hysterical indifference to logic and are divorced from reality.

"She means what she says," he informed me. "We both do. But you have every right to stay out of this if you want to."

"I know him better than that." Emma looked up at me from her kneeling position. "Don't I, darling? You're always telling me how much you love me. Here's your chance to prove it!"

"What the hell are you talking about?" I objected. "Prove that I love you by going to jail for five years?"

She climbed to her feet, stood on her toes and kissed me lightly on the forehead.

"Nobody's going to jail. Apart from Legge no harm will come to anyone."

There was something chilling about

her gaiety. I loosened the neck of my sweater. This was blackmail but I couldn't let her run amok without at least trying to look after her.

"Ok," I said, trying to bring sense to at least one of them, "let's go at it in another way. What exactly do we do with Legge once you've abducted him?"

"*We've* abducted him," Emma corrected smoothly.

Shane lighted a cigarette, his fingers nervous as he made his points.

"We're going to make him print a statement in his newspaper, a recantation."

"A recantation."

"That's right. An admission that he's used his column for personal ends. I'm going to force him to admit that he's lied and blackmailed, betrayed one confidence after another. People have tried to set him up before but he's had the laugh on them all. People seem to be afraid of him. He's got to be stopped somehow."

I listened in amazement as the girl who shares my life and occasionally darns my socks came on sounding like Madame Lefarge at the tumbrils.

"Otherwise he's just going to go on fucking up people's lives. Imagine what happens if we give the story to one of his rivals, another gossip columnist."

"Imagine him cutting his own throat," I objected. "One's as likely as the other. He's not going to give you any goddam statement. It's tantamount to committing professional *hara-kiri*."

"That's what it's meant to be," said Shane. A window cleaner was putting up his ladder across the street and Shane partly drew the curtain, putting us out of the guy's sight. The implications were strangely disturbing. "He's a bully and a coward," Shane said turning and coming back towards me, wagging his finger. "If he thinks his life is in danger he's going to want to save it."

The room was suddenly oppressively

hot and I loosened the neck of my sweater.

"His life's in danger?"

"Don't keep repeating things," Emma said from the kitchen.

I waited till she was in the sitting room again. "Correct me if I'm wrong," I said. "But I get the feeling you people have had this bullshit in mind for some time."

"Right." Shane's eyes were crazy but steady. "I've thought of nothing else since Sara's death. What happened yesterday was the last straw. I'm going to take care of this bastard."

Looking at Emma, I remembered their meetings, the ones she always claimed were connected with settling Sara's affairs.

"I didn't want to worry you," she said quietly.

I had to laugh. It was obvious that she believed what she was saying.

"It's true," she insisted. "I didn't want to involve you."

"Every breath you take involves me,"

I answered. It was too early in the morning to smoke but I lighted a *Celtique*. "Thanks for nothing," I said to Shane. "I thought you were a friend."

"Don't blame Shane," Emma put in quickly. "Blame me. It was my idea in the first place. As a matter of fact we were going to do this weeks ago. I'd worked out a plan. Then Shane was arrested."

She gave the carpet a final wipe and climbed to her feet. "Look, Legge lives in a block that has a basement garage. He leaves his car there. What we do is wait there for him then take him somewhere safe, a place that Shane knows."

"I don't believe it," I said. "I *can't* believe it. What are we going to do, wear nylon stockings over our heads?"

"Animal masks," she said coolly. "They cover the whole of your head. I got them a long time ago."

There was something frightening about her lack of emotion. This was *kidnapping* she was talking about but she made it sound like a shopping expedition.

"Jesus God," I said. "You mean you're really serious about this ridiculous caper?"

"It isn't ridiculous," Shane put in dangerously. "It has to be done and what's more it'll work."

I dragged smoke into my lungs, forgetting the warning about lung cancer printed on the side of the packet.

"I think I'm being had," I said. "You're telling me that we're supposed to turn up in Legge's basement wearing jungle masks and expect him to walk off into the night with us? Is that all there is to it or can we expect a modicum of violence?"

"He'll come." Shane drew the curtain further and opened his desk. He took a small handgun from a drawer inside. "When he sees this he'll come."

"It's only a replica. You can buy them in Marylebone Lane." Emma's explanation was a little too glib to be accurate.

I held out my hand. "Let me see that thing."

He surrendered it reluctantly. It was a Belgian-made automatic and the clip was loaded.

"You must be out of your minds."

He put the gun back in a drawer. Emma answered for both of them.

"Don't be an old woman, Jamie. Nobody's going to shoot him."

"I wish to God I was an old woman," I said wearily. "At least I wouldn't be mixed up in a criminal conspiracy."

She reached up on her toes and ruffled my hair. "We need your aid and assistance, my darling."

"Take the first plane out of the country," I said promptly.

"Legge's *scum*," said Shane. He sounded like some demented revivalist. "You know the description of a gossip-columnist. Someone with ratlike cunning, a plausible manner and very little literary ability. That *is* Legge."

"You've got the quote right," I said. "But the man happened to be talking about journalists not gossip-columnists."

He stared me down. "So?"

Emma took it up. "The thing is, Jamie. We have to know your intentions."

"My intentions!" I put the sofa between us. "That's great, isn't it? You wake me up, stick a hatchet in my hand and tell me to use it to prove my love for you. What the hell do you want from me, Emma? What am I *supposed* to say?"

She wasn't giving an inch. "What you intend to do."

"You know what I'm going to do," I replied. "You must have known from the start and it's nothing short of blackmail."

Shane was over by the fish tank, content for the moment to let Emma do the talking. She probably thought with reason that she would do a better job handling me than he would. The truth was that I knew far more about her than I did about him and one thing was certain: there was nothing that I could do or say that would steer her off her chosen course.

"Ok," she said. "You've heard our plan in the rough. What do you think?"

"It stinks. If someone like Legge disappears people are going to start looking for him. He's got staff, deadlines to meet, a hundred reasons why an alarm should go off the moment he vanishes."

"Wrong," she said coolly. "That's nonsense for a start. Legge lives alone and his office staff never seem to know where he is. I've called there half-a-dozen times. It's hardly surprising since most of the time he's under someone's bed." She was pacing up and down, wafting *Calèche* every time she passed me. "In any case we're only going to keep him a couple of days."

I tried to remember what I'd heard or read about kidnapping and it worried me stiff.

"Put it this way. Let's assume that he is missed and that there is an alarm. The police will be out asking people to remember unimportant details like whether the neighbours are acting strangely, a variation of pattern. *This* kind of thing!" I crossed the room and opened up the curtains. "If we go through with this we'll be at one another's throats before it's over."

Shane looked back from the fish tank. "There'll be no one to see him. We're putting him seventy-five feet under the ground."

"Seventy-five feet? Where?" I demanded.

"I'll show you later." He came across to the sofa. "Look, Jamie, Legge follows the same routine in the evening four or five days a week. At least we know this. He drives his car to Fulham and plays squash for half-an-hour or so. He drives home, leaves his car in the basement, goes upstairs and changes. Then he starts out again on his rounds, leaving his car. He uses cabs."

He spoke with the certainty of someone with superior knowledge. "How do you know all this stuff?" I asked.

He nodded across at Emma. "She's been checking it out for the last month."

"Great!" I commented, sticking my hands on my knees. "So that's where you were. So much for the pottery lessons or whatever it was supposed to be. You realize of course that I'll never trust you again."

"It's the price I have to pay," she said, narrowing her eyes and shortening the band of freckles across her nose. She seemed to be treating the whole thing as some sort of prank, at least part of the time. Shane was much tenser, acting as if he understood the implications of what he was planning. It didn't stop him from a confidence that for me bordered on lunacy.

I shook my head. "You people are making it all sound too easy. At best it isn't going to be the way you see it. Your scheme's based on a false premise."

"Is that right?" Emma cocked her head at me.

I ignored the note of sarcasm. "Let me get it straight. We're not going to clobber Legge. The only force used is what'll be necessary. What you propose to do is lock him up somewhere till he signs the sort of statement you want."

"That's it," said Shane.

"He won't do it." I was sure that he wouldn't, too.

"He'll do it." Shane's voice had become flat and menacing like a missionary threatening a sinner with the flames of hell. "At the end of twenty-four hours where he's going he'll be ready to sign anything."

Emma slipped in behind the sofa and kissed me on top of the head.

I seemed to be getting much more than my ration.

"He doesn't have a single friend in Fleet Street, Jamie. All the other vultures are just waiting for the chance to tear him to pieces."

I pulled her down by the arms, bringing her face close to mine. Whatever I was going to do was for her not for him.

"You haven't thought this thing through, baby. Hasn't it occurred to you that Legge knows the three of us? He knows our faces and our voices."

"He won't recognize those," Shane said promptly. "He can *guess* who we are, I'll grant you that but he'll never be able to prove it."

"We're going to be each others alibis," Emma said smugly.

I shook my head in despair. Things got worse every time she opened her mouth.

"Come downstairs with me," Shane said mysteriously. There are a couple of offices and a washroom on the first storey of the house. Shane has done the same sort of alterations down there as he had in his apartment. Large picture windows offered a view of hoar-frosted turf, some blackened trees and a stone lion that had come from their parents' home. He unlocked a drawer in the Habitat desk and shoved a green file across at me.

"Take a look at that."

I did. It was a picture of business premises, a four-storey building that angled a corner site. There was a bank, a dry cleaner and delicatessen and an empty store with one of Shane's agency boards hanging outside. THESE PREMISES TO LET. His finger moved sideways from the empty store to what looked like massive sliding doors. These were shut tight.

"Do you see anything there that you recognize?" he demanded. He couldn't have been drinking yet he was strangely cranked-up.

I studied the picture more closely. A sign over the panelled wood doors was almost illegible, half of the letters missing.

ND GR UND

I nodded. A number of London

Underground stations had been closed at the end of the war because of bomb-damage. Others had been abandoned as the lines were rerouted. These stations were deep below the surface, bypassed and often completely forgotten. He put the picture back in its folder and locked it away in the desk.

"That's the entrance to a disused station in Highgate and it's been closed for thirty-two years. That shop you saw with my board outside used to be a tobacconist's. There's an entrance into the booking-hall and I have the keys."

His plan began to make sense. At least this part of it did. He checked the time by the clock on the wall.

"We'd better get out of here. It's almost ten and sometimes Amanda comes early."

Upstairs Emma was sitting on the sofa with her legs tucked up under her, filing her nails. She cocked her head as we came into the room.

"Satisfied?"

"As satisfied as anyone can be who's

on his way to jail," I replied.

"You're paranoid," she answered tartly. "There's not the slightest chance of anyone going to jail. We turn Legge loose once he's signed what we want and Shane and I sleep better. That's all there is to it."

I was near enough for her to touch her lips with her fingers and lay them on my mouth.

"And you'll sleep better too if you behave yourself."

I could hear my voice, strangely hoarse. "And when are you going to require my services?"

They exchanged a conspiratorial glance. "Probably tonight. If not tonight then tomorrow or the next day. We take our chances till we're successful. Everything's ready."

They were in earnest about getting hold of Legge that night and we talked about it for the next hour or so. The window-cleaner took his ladder off somewhere else. Amanda arrived and the house-phone rang.

Shane ignored it, talking quietly in a monotone, flicking his fingers to make his points. There was to be a joint alibi that would stay the same for every night as long as we needed it. We would meet at Shane's, ostensibly staying for a meal and playing cards and Zilch until the small hours of the following morning. With any sort of luck one of the neighbours would see Emma and me arrive and remember the Jaguar being left parked outside Shane's house. He'd gone as far as planning menus for the next few days and studying the television programmes so that we'd have the correct answers for any questions that might be asked. The animal masks that Emma had bought turned out to be hidden in our garage. I was by no means certain that I liked this new and devious side to her character.

The plan was for us to slip out of the Lennox Gardens house through a door in the wall at the end of the garden, emerging a block away.

Shane explained that there'd be no problem about transport since we'd be using Legge's own car to take him to Highgate. We were going to leave him in the disused station and return to Shane's house by way of the garden door. When the time came for Emma and me to leave we'd have to make sure that our adieux were noticed. As Shane pointed out, nothing sticks in the mind of a bad sleeper like the sound of a car door slammed hard at one o'clock in the morning.

The house-phone rang again. This time Shane took the call. He talked for a moment and replaced the receiver.

"I have to go. Amanda's just reminded me that I've got an eleven o'clock appointment. I'll see you here at six o'clock."

Emma put her arms around him. "Don't forget to go to Highgate and make sure that everything's in order."

"I'll go there this afternoon," he answered and gave me his hand. "Thanks for everything, Jamie. I knew

I could count on you."

I drove back through the park and stopped near the bridge that crosses the Serpentine. The windruffled water was reflecting the rays of the pale sun overhead. I opened the door on my side.

"You drive. I'll see you at home."

She slid into my place and hitched the seat nearer the wheel. "Where are you going?"

"I'm taking a walk," I answered. "You two aren't the only people who need to think."

She adjusted her gloves and smiled. Her voice had an edge. "Well don't think too much. This means an awful lot to me, Jamie."

Our eyes locked. "It means an awful lot to me, too. That's why *I* have to think."

She was going to reply but thought better of it, just ramming into low gear and taking off fast. I wandered down past the restaurant and under the bridge by the edge of the water where we fed the geese and the ducks in the winter.

They followed me now, honking, but my mind was on other things. There was no warmth at all in the sun and the few people in the park seemed to be doing no more than getting from one place to another as fast as they could. I found an empty chair near the sad remains of a great tree ravaged by Dutch elm disease and lighted a cigarette. It was time to take stock. I had been in England for almost ten years, a fugitive from a Southern Ontario fruitfarm. My grandfather with whom I lived ran out of time one winter's evening and there was nothing to hold me in Canada any longer. My parents had been divorced when I was five, my mother long gone, God alone knew where. My father was living in Southern California with a girl half his age and running an antique shop. We exchanged ritual letters once or twice a year. We'd never been close. Even for the few years I spent with him as a child I'd found most of his attitudes false and his wisdom doubtful.

I sold Gramp's two hundred and eighty fruitful acres and the old white house for good money and invested in Alberta oilstock. It didn't make me rich but I could afford to pick and choose. I came to Europe, studied at R.A.D.A. for a year and served another three in places like Bath, Bolton and Malvern, carrying spears in repertory companies. I had enough money not to worry about the miserable salaries and saw myself as a latterday Olivier. A friendly manager in the business took me aside one wet Sunday with the rain sliding off Welsh slate roofs and told me the facts of life. I wasn't an actor nor would I ever make one. I think I heard the news with a sense of relief. I finished the week out, travelled back to London first class and started the stunt agency. I worked it up gradually, using the people I liked till I had a great team of guys and girls on the books. We achieved a reputation for being professional and reliable though expensive. It was a good living and one way and another I was doing most of the things I wanted to do. Now all this was to be put in jeopardy.

I had knocked around at home in Canada as well as in Europe but I'd never been in the hands of the police. The idea made my toes curl. I didn't blame Emma and Shane as much as Legge yet the thought of dealing with him in the way they'd come up with scared the shit out of me. The more I thought about it, the deeper the hole I was in. I even considered making an anonymous phone call to Legge, putting him on his guard. But I knew that if I did this I'd never be able to live with myself.

I walked on past the statue of Peter Pan, deserted now as was the rest of the park, and finally my mind was made up. It was too late for me to back out. I could only keep my fingers crossed and my passport handy. I visited a travel agency and my bank on the way home, buying a couple of open flights to Rome and drew out a large sum in cash. It was a strange sensation. I was starting to feel like a fugitive. When I reached the mews I found that Emma had put the car away. I smelled the corned beef hash frying as soon as I opened the front door. Emma must have stopped off at a supermarket because there were bottles of Budweiser on the kitchen table. She turned from the stove as I entered the room, reached up in her stockinged feet and kissed me yet another time.

I've learned a lot about myself through Emma, principally about my weaknesses. Not that I did anything about them but I saw myself through someone else's eyes maybe for the first time in my life. She was a hell of a lot different to the succession of Sloane Rangers who had been her predecessors, harpies bent on getting far more than they gave.

The hash was a rich brown and she'd put apples and capers in it.

"I'm really getting the treatment today," I kidded.

She cracked a couple of eggs and slid them into the poacher, grease on her nose and her hair wispy from the heat of the stove.

"Come on, now!" I challenged. "My favourite food and beer!"

She spread a checked cloth over the table and spooned the smoking hash onto the plates.

"Did you get your thinking done?"

She's a good cook. Even my grandmother would have approved.

"I did," I said with my mouth full. "And I went to the bank and drew out two hundred and fifty each in cash. I'm keeping it here in case we have to move in a hurry." I showed her the tickets I'd bought.

She forked food into her mouth, looking down her short nose at me.

"You worry too much, Jamie. If I didn't know you better I'd have doubts about you."

"Be my guest," I answered. "Have

all the doubts you want if they deal with the matter of my courage. *I* am scared rigid."

She was silent for a while and I glanced across the mews. The girl who lives opposite was shaking something out of the window. She's a fresh-air fiend who's forever shaking and polishing. She spends a lot of the time running around the house naked but I'd never seen a man in there.

"Bad luck," said Emma. "She's got her clothes on."

I tried to look superior but failed. She tipped what was left on her plate into the waste-disposer. Then she pulled her chair round to my side of the table and leaned her head on my shoulder. There are lights in her hair that put me in mind of maple trees in the autumn.

"Shane's got it all worked out," she assured me. "And when it's over there'll be one less bastard in Fleet Street. No more, no less."

I wanted to believe it. Her closeness and confidence helped but I still had the feeling that there was something basically wrong with the scheme, not with the moral issues involved as much as its feasibility. Yet there was only one way left for me to go and that was forward. I washed up the plates and pans. By the time I'd finished, Emma had her portable typewriter on the sitting room table and was answering the morning's mail. I slipped off my shoes and lay down on the bed, hoping that something would happen between then and nightfall. Something like Legge being sent on assignment to China or dropping dead, anything that would get me off the hook I was wriggling on.

I must have dozed. It was four-thirty by the bedside clock when Emma brought in a tray with tea and toast. It was almost dark outside and she drew the curtains. I could see the neat pile of letters on the little table at the head of the stairs. She had changed into an old pair of ski pants and a black anorak. I finished my tea and tied my sneakers.

She lifted a shopping bag onto the bed and displayed the contents. She had brought the animals' masks up from the garage, a couple of foxes' heads and an ape's. They were plastic moulded and light. I put one on and looked at myself in the mirror, seeing a barnyard villain from a Disney cartoon. I emptied my pockets of everything except for my keys and my money. I must have seen it somewhere or read about it, the professional rogue preparing for a piece of villainy, no identification carried, only essentials. I set the fire going and banked it with coal. My last act was to stand the screen in front of the fireplace. There was something reassuring about the chore, a promise to myself that I would be back to find that nothing had changed.

The street lamps were burning by the time we reached Lennox Gardens. There was a place to park not too far away from Shane's house. The front door of the house opposite was wide open, a man in a fisherman's sweater pulling an elderly bulldog along the railings. He may not have noticed us getting out of the car and going up the steps to ring Shane's doorbell. But he turned, nodding a greeting as Shane opened up. The offices on the first floor were closed, Amanda had evidently gone home for the night. We followed Shane upstairs. He was wearing rubbersoled shoes, dark pants and a leather jacket and was whistling tonelessly. The blinds were down in the lighted sitting room, the Zilch dice out on the throwing-board. Shane's preparations were certainly thorough. According to the score recorded on a pad I had won a couple of pounds at the end of the evening's play.

He looked at me with the same directness of gaze he had used on Legge in the courtroom. It was a kind of assessment as if he was searching for signs of hidden weaknesses. The assumption that I couldn't play his goddam game irritated me. The feeling wasn't helped by Emma's remark.

"Don't worry about Jamie," she said, propped on the end of the sofa. "Jamie's fine."

I felt the back of my neck beginning to redden and I raised my hand.

"Hold it right there!" I waited till I had their undivided attention. "Now you two listen to me. Jamie doesn't approve but Jamie isn't going to fold on you. Worry about yourselves not me."

A smile leaked over Shane's narrow freckled face. "We know that, don't get up tight. Take a look at this."

He handed me something that felt like an iron ring wrapped in burlap sacking. I weighed it in my hand, shrugged and gave it back to him. He slipped behind me quickly, holding the iron hoop high above my head. It fell before I knew what was happening, carrying the sack down with it as far as my knees. The closed end of the sack rested on top of my head, imprisoning my arms against my sides as effectively as if I'd been in a straitjacket. I could see nothing at all through the burlap.

Shane lifted the sack from my head. "Ok. Now try it on me."

I got it together at the second attempt. Once the iron hoop was down past his shoulders it was all over. Shane put the sack in the shopping bag with the animal masks.

"That'll be your job," he said. "You can't miss as long as you come from behind. I'll keep him occupied."

He dragged the television trolley near the windows, switched on the set with the volume low. The flickering lights on the screen showed on the blinds. Anyone on the street below would gather an impression of movement in the room. Shane unlocked his desk, still whistling out of tune and stuck the small Belgian automatic in his trouser top.

"I was out at Highgate this afternoon. Everything's in order. I even oiled the locks. I've rigged something up down below, something that will hold the bastard."

Emma turned her wrist. "It's twenty-five to six. Time we made a move." She took the phone off the hook and said to Shane, "If anyone calls they'll get the engaged signal. Either that or they'll think the number's out-of-order."

"Good thinking," said Shane. "Now you know what you have to do when we get there. Jamie gets that sack over his head as quickly as possible and Emma drives. If there's anyone around, any sort of danger, we simply take the lift up and walk out through the front entrance. And try again tomorrow night."

Emma put her word in. "Keep quiet going across the gardens." She was the one who was doing most talking but I didn't bother to point this out.

Shane opened the door at the top of the stairs and we went down in Indian file. Emma and I waited in the darkened hallway while Shane unfastened the door to the garden. It was much colder outside, no wind and a sliver of moon on its back in the sky. The houses on each side were sealed for the night and the only sound was that of the distant traffic. Shane led us over stiffening turf and through the door at the end of the garden. There was no one to see us come out.

We hailed a cruising cab that took us as far as Regent's Park where Shane paid him off. We walked the quarter of a mile to Legge's block of flats, an ornate building with floodlit fountains in front. An entrance ramp on one side of the block sloped down to the subterranean garage. The exit ramp was on the opposite side. There was no service, no gas pumps, nothing but straight parking space. We hung around in somebody's gateway while Emma walked down the ramp. She was back almost immediately, beckoning us across the street. The way she did it was completely professional. Anyone watching would have thought she was stroking her hair. She'd certainly taken to crime. I had to keep reminding myself that Legge was responsible for the death of their sister. Otherwise none of this even began to make sense.

The underground garage was the size of a football pitch with the ceiling buttressed by concrete pillars that cast long shadows. There were four lifts, one serving each side of the building.

Emma piloted us through lines of parked cars as far as the west wall and pointed out the index numbers stencilled on the oilstained floor.

"That's Legge's space."

We were standing no more than a dozen feet from the lift shaft. Shane brought the cage down and we stepped inside, holding the cage by leaving one of the gates open. We could see the entrance ramp clearly. My stomach was starting to give me some trouble. A small black car rolled down from the street, driven by a woman. She went upstairs, using the lift opposite. Shane tapped the face of his watch with a fingernail. Emma produced the animal masks from the shopping-bag. She didn't appear to have lost an ounce of her nerve. We slipped the masks over our heads and she gave me the sack. Shane's gun was in his gloved hand. He and I were facing the doorway, Emma to one side.

A large blue Dodge surged down the ramp and headed straight for us, the mutter from its tailpipe echoing in the confined space. Shane lifted his hand as the sound of the motor died. A coach-built click followed. I could just about see Legge, his suntan accentuated by a pale-green sweater. He was stretching his arms and legs, relaxed like a big brown bear.

I braced myself as Legge came towards us and slid back the lift doors. He stopped dead, seeing the gun in Shane's fist. I shall never forget the look on his face. It was far more than fear. There was an element of guilt, as though he accepted the fact that retribution had finally caught up with him. Emma was the first to move.

She snatched Legge's car-keys from his grasp so quickly that there was no time for him to take avoiding action. I came at him from behind, dropping the hoop-weighted sack over his head just as he opened his mouth. He let out one stifled yell that chased itself round the basement and then stood quite still.

The worst moment was getting him from the lift to the Dodge. Miraculously there was nobody else in the garage and Emma already had the trunk of the car open. Legge put up no fight as Shane and I half-shoved, half-dragged, him towards it. We heaved him into the trunk and I leaned hard with my hundred and eighty pounds, forcing him down. His body jack-knifed awkwardly, three-quarters of it held in the sack. His hooded head was resting on the spare wheel.

I slammed the lid of the trunk down and tore off the fox's mask. I was sweating heavily. The other two were already in the car, Emma at the wheel,

Shane sitting beside her. I climbed in behind and stuffed the three masks back in the shopping bag. Emma hit the starter, her chin lifting as the powerful car coasted up the slope to the street. Nobody spoke. It was fine with me. My heart was banging so loudly that I wouldn't have been too sure about my voice. Now that the preliminaries were over I couldn't help thinking about all the things that could have gone wrong. The possibilities seemed endless. Somehow it didn't help that so far the plan had succeeded.

We headed north in the direction of Chalk Farm and on to Haverstock Hill. Emma was driving like a schoolmistress taking her test so what happened next was totally unexpected. A taxi pulled out of a side street immediately in front of us. Emma stepped on the brakes, managing to pull the Dodge to a complete stop, leaving no more than the thickness of a playing card between the two vehicles. The hack was out of his taxi in a flash, a burly character in a red plaid cap and with a combative manner. The headlamps of the Dodge were glaring at the rear end of the taxi. He bent down, inspecting the body and paintwork narrowly.

"Drive on!" Shane said quietly.

"Stay where you are!" I countered, my fingers digging into Emma's shoulder.

I could see the microphone bracket hanging over the front seat of the taxi. The cab was radio-controlled. We'd be on the air before we'd travelled a couple of hundred yards. Emma was fumbling for the button that worked the electric window on her side. I found it for her. "Be nice," I warned as the window lowered.

The cabdriver lumbered over displaying the aggrieved self-righteousness of his kind.

"What are you supposed to be doing? You bleedin' near caused an accident there!"

"Nonsense," said Emma.

A loud thud came from the trunk

106

as if Legge had guessed what was happening and was trying to call for help. Either the cabdriver misjudged the sound or he didn't hear it. Maybe he was too carried away with his own production.

"How long have you been driving?" he demanded, lifting his chin.

"Long enough to learn how to drive properly," answered Emma.

"*Drive properly!*" The cabdriver's expression was scornful. "I'm not a bloody mind-reader, you know!"

"You don't have to be," Emma retorted. "All you have to do is observe the rules of the road, such as coming to a complete stop when a sign tells you to. Now will you please get out of my way."

The hack stepped back sharply, a look of astonishment replacing his hectoring manner. More thuds came from the trunks as Emma drove off. She held her speed down, challenging me in the rearview mirror.

"Why are you looking like that,

Jamie? *What's the matter?*"

I glanced back through the window but the taxi had driven off in the opposite direction.

"Nothing," I answered sarcastically. "Nothing at all. All we needed is a good lively argument with a gimp like that and the police called in as referees. I'm sure you can handle the situation. What's the matter!" I repeated bitterly.

"Come on, there's no harm done," said Shane, making peace.

I changed the subject. "You'd better do something about our friend's feet."

"I will," Shane said shortly.

We went on for about a mile, turning off at his direction into a quiet neighbourhood of small self-contained houses, all of them with gardens. The streets were deserted. I recognized the corner-site from the photograph Shane had shown me, the agency board hanging outside the empty premises. It was a well-chosen location from our point of view. The small shopping complex served a surburban area that was five or six hundred feet up. Beneath us was the dark expanse of Highgate Golf Course.

Widely-spaced streetlamps stood sentinel over stretches of empty pavement. Some of the shop-fronts were lighted. The travel agency offered coloured views of Brazil to a non-existent audience. It was a friendly neighbourhood where morning shoppers would gossip in the sun, collect their children from school and do their morning shopping. A backwater in the mainstream. At seven o'clock at night the front doors were shut, the cats out, the dogs in, the lonely streets left to themselves.

"Here," said Shane.

Emma pulled over to the kerb. We had stopped in front of the tobacconist's. Shane slipped out, glanced right and left and stuck a key in the top lock. He turned a second key and nodded at us. Emma held the lid of the trunk as I hauled Legge upright. He grunted a couple of times and muttered something inaudible. Shane had the shop door open by now. We dragged Legge into the shop between us as Emma moved the Dodge further down the road. She came running back. Shane secured the entrance from the street and opened an inner door that led to the disused booking hall. The tobacconist's had once been used by commuters.

Shane picked a flash from the ground. A second later a powerful beam picked out the brickwork that had been constructed behind the steel sliding doors that sealed the station entrance. The floor was littered with trash. A cat's head grinned from its desiccated body. The light travelled past the closed ticket office, the useless elevators, on to the top of an emergency stairway.

Shane took us to its head and handed the flash to Emma. It isn't easy at the best of times to control a man who has his head in a sack and whose movements are restricted, still less when you are trying to negotiate an iron spiral staircase.

Shane went first, taking some of Legge's weight while I tried to keep him on balance. I counted a hundred and fifty-seven iron treads before we reached bottom. The first thing I noticed down there was the smell. It was the dank smell that you find in caves and old churches, compiled of disuse and moisture. Whatever ventilation there was came through the elevator shafts. The real ventilation ducts had long since been sealed. By the time the air reached the end of its journey it was lifeless and flat.

The light shifted in Emma's hand and something scurried away in the darkness. There were two platforms, one for northbound traffic, the other for southbound. Shane signalled Emma to go to the left. The flashlight beam travelled past faded advertisements that featured products long since forgotten. Both ends of the tunnel had been sealed with bricks about fifty yards from the exits. The lines that lay beyond must have been diverted to bypass the station. I was walking behind Legge, holding him by the shoulders and steering him. His head jerked under the sack as a train rumbled in the distance and I knew that everything was registering. I could imagine how he was feeling, jumped by masked strangers, stuffed into the back of his own car and dragged down into the bowels of the earth. He couldn't see anything, had no idea what was happening and worst of all there was no communication. We hadn't spoken since we pulled him out of the car. Not that I had any sympathy for him. The bastard had been twisting other people's nerve-ends for too long.

The rumbling train vanished in the distance and the silence was unbroken except for the dripping of water from the tunnel roof. Our elongated shadows were grotesque on the ceiling as we moved along the platform. Somewhere near the end Shane suddenly bent down. The steel links of a pair of handcuffs winked in the light. Shane squatted quickly and cuffed Legge's ankles together. Then he motioned me to raise the iron hoop as far as Legge's elbows and hold it there. He grabbed Legge's hands, forced them behind and secured them with a second pair of cuffs. The light went out and I felt the sack being lifted over Legge's head. His body lurched sideways and he fell, tripped by Shane.

Emma's hand found mine in the darkness and we tiptoed away towards the spiral staircase. When we were halfway along the platform an echoing shout followed.

"Stafford!"

We started running, the three of us, our rubbersoled shoes making no sound. Legge's voice chased us,

"I know it's you, Stafford. You're not going to get away with this!"

He was still shouting by the time we reached the staircase. We were halfway up before his voice finally faded. We made our exit through the shop to the street. Shane locked up carefully. The street was empty as we made our way back to the car. I climbed in the back and lighted a cigarette with shaking fingers.

"What happens now?" I demanded. "How do you think you're going to get him to sign anything?"

Shane turned, swinging the handcuff keys between thumb and forefinger.

"He'll sign. After a night down there he'll sign his grandmother's death-warrant."

We were all sweating, including Emma. "Did you hear those rats?" she asked, her tone almost smug. And this from a girl who runs if she as much as sees mice shit.

Both of them seemed to be ignoring the fact that Legge had identified Shane. I reminded them of it.

"He knows who you are and he doesn't have to be clairvoyant to know who *we* are!"

Shane stretched comfortably. "Bollix.

We're home and dried, Jamie. I don't give a fuck what Legge *thinks* he knows. It's proving it that's going to count. You'll find that our friend won't be quite so hardnosed tomorrow."

It was almost nine o'clock when we reached Regent's Park. Returning Legge's car was a crucial move and I didn't like the idea of Emma going on show again.

"Why don't you let me do it?" I pleaded.

She was her usual obstinate self. "If there's the slightest danger — if I as much as suspect there is — I shall just keep going and straight up the other ramp."

She stopped across the street from Legge's flat. The Dodge tail-lights vanished. We were standing in the shadow of somebody's gatepost. I could see Shane's face and he was smiling. I had a sudden rush of blood to the head. There was no way I could have stopped myself.

"What the hell do you think you've

done to look so goddam pleased with yourself?" I demanded. "Why didn't you pull this thing solo if it means so much to you? Why involve Emma? Why involve me?"

He suspended his toneless whistling, one eye on the exit ramp.

"Emma didn't need to be involved. This is family. As a matter of fact I wish you'd kept out of it. You've done nothing but complain from the very first moment."

The tenseness was broken by Emma's appearance. She came from the entrance-hall and hurried across the lighted forecourt. She linked her arms with ours, one of us on each side of her.

"I left the car in his parking space and took the lift up. Nobody saw me leave, not even the porter."

She sounded like a small girl who has just won some nursery victory, delighted with herself and strangely innocent. We found a cab to take us back to Knightsbridge, negotiated the door at the end of the garden and went up into the warmth of Shane's sitting room. He turned off the television set and raised the blinds for the world to see in. The smile was back on his face but his eyes were oddly restive. "Anyone like a drink?"

"A scotch," I said. I didn't like his brand but at that moment I'd have drunk anything. I moved in front of the mirror, looking for the white hairs I was sure I would find.

He put the gun back in the desk and locked the drawer. "Now about tomorrow," he started, rubbing a hand through his red thatch.

I shook my head quickly. "Don't look for me tomorrow. It's the end of the line for me."

He turned from the drinks table, a vodka-tonic in his hand. "But that's when I'll need you most, Jamie."

He was Emma's brother and he'd been through a lot but my mood was to dump him.

"That's not what you said half-an-hour ago," I retorted. "Why don't you tell Emma what you said?"

"She already knows how I feel," he said grinning. "As a matter of fact if it hadn't been for Emma you wouldn't have been on square one. It isn't a question of likes or dislikes, trust or no trust, Jamie. It's a question of expediency."

I looked across at Emma. "Thanks a lot."

She made a little face. "I love you," she said as if that explained everything. But I was glad that he'd heard her say it.

"Since you're in," added Shane. "You're going to have to do your share."

I shook my head again. "Not tomorrow, I don't." The words dropped like stones on wet felt.

Both of them challenged at the same time. "Why?"

I looked at Emma. "Because it happens to be a day when I'm working and I'm responsible for three other people's livelihood, remember?"

She covered her mouth with her fingers. "My God, that's right! Thames Television!"

"Thames Television," I agreed. "At eight o'clock in the morning."

Shane's hand dismissed me. "It doesn't matter, Emma. You and I can do whatever's necessary."

He moved to the window with his glass in his hand. The man living opposite had a permanent interest in Shane's activities and Shane obliged him now. I finished my drink and motioned to Emma.

"We'd better go, honey. I'll need an early call."

She loped close to Shane and whispered something in his ear. Only the last of what she said was audible.

"What time do you want me here?"

"Eleven-thirty," he answered. "And the *Turk's Head* not here." It was the name of a neighbourhood pub that we all used.

He offered me his hand, the Cavalier once again. "I meant everything that

I said, Jamie, but it doesn't stop me being grateful for all that you've done. Thanks."

"I meant what I said too," I retorted. "I think your scheme's crazy and I want no further part of it."

He smiled his charming smile, his eyes secret, but he made no answer. He came as far as the street door with us, holding the goodnight scene for his neighbour opposite. We were halfway across Hyde Park when I said what had been on my mind ever since we left Shane's place.

"You're not meeting Shane tomorrow and don't give me a hard time over it. I want you out of the goddam caper. I want us *both* out of it."

The shadows beyond the park lamps were deep and dark. Emma answered in a voice that was new to me, a voice as final and positive as the sound of a bank-vault shutting.

"If you say one more word or try to stop me I'll leave you and never come back. I mean that, Jamie."

I glanced sideways. We had reached Bayswater Road and were waiting for the signals to change. She was staring straight ahead through the windshield.

"I don't believe you," I said. There was more hope than conviction in the statement.

She turned her head towards me very slowly, her small face closed.

"Just don't try me, Jamie. *Please* don't try me!"

I wasn't about to do so. Her intentions were plain. The signals went green and I shifted gears.

"What the hell's happening to us, Emma?" I asked.

I sensed her shoulders move. "You're learning about family loyalties, Jamie. No more, no less."

We drove the rest of the way home without speaking. The mews was empty and inhospitable. Emma opened the garage doors for me and hurried upstairs. By the time I joined her she had made sandwiches and left them on the kitchen table with a couple of bottles of beer. I ate standing, depressed by her refusal to appreciate my concern for her. The last thing I wanted to do was fight. But her mood had changed completely when I went into the bedroom. She was wearing the top half of my pyjamas and sipping a glass of hot milk. She smiled and it was the Emma I knew again. I brushed my teeth and got in beside her.

Television was lousy and I read Pepys for a while while she leafed through *Vogue*. Suddenly she reached across me without warning and put out the light. I felt her climb onto me, her mouth seeking mine, her hand between my legs. I smelled the warm biscuit smell of her armpits. When it was all over, we lay there spent, each within the framework of his private thoughts. Her voice came in a tiny whisper.

"I do love you, Jamie. Remember that whatever happens."

I found her hand. "I need it."

Her lips nuzzled my shoulder. "Goodnight, my darling."

"Goodnight," I replied and held her as tight as I could.

She was still sleeping when the alarm went off in the morning. It was six-fifteen. I groped for the button and stifled the clock. There was a drive of an hour to reach the studios where I was supposed to pick up the rest of my crew. We were shooting on location, somewhere near the airport in a network of man-made lakes and gravel pits. I dressed in the darkness and shaved by touch. I drank my tea in the kitchen and left a note for her on the table.

I love you too so take great care!

I wanted to say more but I didn't know what. I could only hope that Shane would take care of her. She was still fast asleep when I peeped round the door with the sheet covering the lower part of her face. Her hair made fox-fire on the pillow. She looked good for another twelve hours. I could hope for nothing better than that she'd go on sleeping and miss her date with Shane. I had this strong feeling that if we somehow managed to get through today without disaster the Legge syndrome would end one way or another. Shane would have to let him go whether he signed the document or not — and probably he wouldn't. I imagined him being turned loose somewhere on Hampstead Heath in the early hours of the morning. As for the rest, I kept telling myself that here at least Shane was right. No matter what Legge might suspect he must know that he hadn't a hope in hell of proving it.

It was an easy drive with not too much traffic and only the first hint of fog to contend with. I parked in the studio-lot and walked across to the administration building. Paul, Sam and Liza were waiting in the Reception area, changed and ready. I collected my clothes from Wardrobe and joined them in the bus that was waiting outside. The camera crew was already playing poker, the actors and actresses stifling yawns. The only people really awake other than the poker-players were the director and the continuity-girl. We started off on our journey with the mobile canteen close behind.

We were shooting a speedboat chase with Paul, Sam, Liza and me playing heavies escaping with the loot having just burned a bank. We were really doubling, the Balaclava helmets and flying spray hiding our faces. The action entailed the overturning of the speedboat. It took them four tries before they got the take right. By then we had been immersed in freezing water for almost half-an-hour. The director was young and painstaking. He was also human. He called a break at noon and they gave us blankets to wrap in, hot soup and ham sandwiches.

I was working on mine when Liza came from the canteen carrying a newspaper. She dropped it in my lap and sat down beside me, huddled in her outsize fisherman's sweater, her short dark hair frizzled with the damp, her eyes curious. It was a copy of the *Globe* with a picture of Legge on the front page, standing beside the Dodge and smiling at the camera. The caption read:

HAS ANYONE SEEN THIS MAN?

The feature-writer went on to explain that Legge had been due at an editorial monthly conference the night before. When he failed to show, the others had called his flat to no purpose. His secretary had taken a cab to Regent's Park. When her assaults on his doorbell had gone unanswered, she had consulted the building manager. Legge's apartment had been opened up with a passkey but no sign of him was found. The garage was checked and his car was found. It was at this moment that his editor-in-chief informed the police. The *Globe* was offering a reward of one thousand pounds.

Is he the victim of one or more of his enemies, the writer demanded, with references to Legge as the People's reporter and the Scourge of the Privileged Classes. And so on.

It was all too close for my comfort. The reward offered wasn't that high but there must have been something behind it. The food I had just eaten suddenly revolted me.

"Isn't that the creep Emma's brother had the court case over?" asked Liza curiously. "It's the same guy, isn't it?"

I stood her off with some kind of answer as Paul came over to join us. He sat down on the tarpaulin spread at the edge of the water, pointing at the copy of the *Globe*.

"There's some taxi-driver who claims to have seen Legge's car last night. Only Legge wasn't supposed to have been in it. It was on Capital Radio. Jack in the canteen heard it."

I just about managed to smile, my voice coming from the far end of the gravel pit.

"*Taxi-driver?*"

He hunched a shoulder and bit deep

into his sandwich. "I don't see what all the fuss is about quite frankly. If a prick like that gets lost so much the better!"

It was a long afternoon. We finished shooting as soon as the light began to fade. Back at the studio, they offered us hot baths that the others took. I declined. The only thing on my mind was getting home as fast as I could. I was on my way out to the car-park when one of the security guards stopped me.

"There's a lady been trying to reach you all afternoon. She must have called five or six times. I told her you were out on location. She did leave her name but I mislaid the slip of paper. But it was a Miss Emma something-or-other, that I do remember."

I thanked him and walked out to the car. It was no good calling her. A phone was useless for what I had to say. I needed to see her face. I drove like a fool, taking chances, my brain trying to deal with what looked like being the complete collapse of our crazy venture. I would have gladly settled if we could have somehow wriggled out of the mess scot free. Shane had to be crazy. Anyone else would have checked out the chance of Legge having an office meeting. It had crossed my mind but by then it was too late. You can't stop halfway down a toboggan run. The news of Legge's vanishing trick was plastered all over the front of his paper and the cabdriver had recognized the car. I didn't want to think about the next step in logic.

The sitting room lights were on in the flat. I left the car in the mews and ran upstairs. Emma was in the sitting room, lying face down on the sofa. There was a bottle of wine on the floor beside her, three-quarters of it gone. I knew immediately that we were in bad trouble. Emma isn't a drinker and certainly not at six in the evening. I turned her over gently. The first thing I saw was the angry-looking swelling on her left cheekbone. I wrapped my arms round her and raised her up.

"What is it, darling? What happened?"

She mumbled something but her mouth was against my sweater and I couldn't hear. I lifted her chin. She either couldn't or wouldn't answer me. I held her at arm's length. Her cheekbone was bruised but the skin wasn't broken.

"Who did this to your face?" I demanded.

She shook her head miserably. She was sober in spite of the wine she had drunk.

"Legge's dead," she said.

My arms dropped to my sides. The words made no sense for a second.

"How do you mean 'dead'?"

Only her lips had colour. The rest of her face was bloodless beneath the freckles. She reached out blindly, the tears suddenly running down her nose, her fingernails digging into my sweater.

"He fell from the platform. His head was smashed in. It was horrible, Jamie."

I closed the sitting room door, poured myself a large scotch and sat down beside her on the sofa. The scotch seared my stomach but it tasted of nothing. She wiped her eyes on her sleeve. I had never seen her like this, scared and miserable and I didn't know how to help her. "Where's Shane?" I demanded.

She gave a little shake of her head. "I don't know. He brought me back here. We were trying to get hold of you."

She winced as I touched her bruised cheek. "Tell me what happened," I said.

The enormity of what she was saying grew with each word, fulfilling the premonition of disaster that I'd had from the beginning. She and Shane had reached Highgate Hill about noon. They'd hung around in the shopping precinct, waiting for a chance to enter the tobacco-store unobserved. The opportunity came during the lunch break. Most of the neighbouring shops closed down for an hour.

"We'd bought some food for him. Some bread, cheese and milk. It was just as dark below even in daytime. The first thing we heard as we reached the bottom of those stairs was Legge's voice calling. 'Stafford?' Just like that. We didn't answer, didn't speak to one another. I was holding the flashlight. Shane had the gun. Legge had managed to drag himself along the platform and was lying there like a wounded animal. He'd wet himself and he stank."

She shivered, closing her eyes for a second. I stuck a lighted cigarette in her fingers. She took a couple of drags and resumed.

"Shane undid his hands but he wouldn't touch the food or the milk."

"Were you wearing those masks again?"

She nodded. "But he knew who we were. He used both our names. He wanted Shane to take him to a loo but Shane kept pushing this paper at him and telling him to sign it. He was screaming, Shane I mean."

"What was on the paper?"

"I didn't read it. Something to do with Sara."

I poured myself another scotch and built on the fire in my stomach. It was difficult to accept that I was party to this kind of violence.

"Legge wouldn't sign. He kept saying that his newspaper would find him, that we wouldn't get away with it. Suddenly Shane lost his temper again and started shouting, telling Legge that if he didn't sign he would blow his head off. The awful thing is that I think he meant it."

I believed her. A guy like Shane can crank himself up to the point where the threat is the act itself.

"And then what?"

"Suddenly everything seemed to change. I don't know whether Legge was acting or not. I suppose he must have been. He started to talk about Sara, how much he had loved her. He accused us for breaking up his affair with her. Well not so much me as

Shane. The odd thing is that Shane didn't bother to deny it. They'd stopped shouting and for a moment or two they were almost friendly. Then Legge said that he'd sign the paper. He said his life was finished in England anyway. He'd lost all his friends. There was an offer of a job in the States. He was going to take it and start all over."

"You mean Legge actually *signed*?" I'd have bet a hundred to one against it.

She moved her head from side to side. "It never came to it. He asked Shane to take him to the loo and Shane unfastened his ankles."

She was silent suddenly as if reliving the scene.

"I can guess," I said quickly. "That's when he started to run. And Shane shot him."

She shook her head again. "I was holding the light on him. He hit me in the face before I knew what was happening. The torch dropped on the ground. By that time he was running down the platform in the darkness. There was a big bang and a flash as Shane fired the gun but he missed. I heard the bullet ricochet. Legge must have stumbled and fallen from the platform. When we got the torch working again, he was lying between the rails with blood everywhere. It was horrible. The back of his head was split wide open."

She looked down at her hands with revulsion. I was stroking her hair mechanically, my mind jumping like a hunted hare. Whichever direction it took, there was one memory that clamoured loudly for recognition. The legal jargon may not have been right but the gist of it went something like this. If x people conspire to commit a felony and as a result of that felony death occurs then x conspirators are equally guilty of murder. And if death was the result of an accident? Try as I may I couldn't make that one sound any better.

"What did you do with the body?"

My voice was as uptight as hers.

She ran the tip of her tongue over her lips. "We left it where it was. We didn't touch it. You'll have to talk to Shane, Jamie. Find out what we're going to do."

There was no time to answer. A car drew up in the mews below. I went to the kitchen window, certain in my bones what I was about to see. Two men were standing in front of our street door, their bodies foreshortened in the light from the carriage lamp. The doorbell rang and the taller of the two men stepped back, looking up at the windows. I made a sign that I was coming down.

"Police," I said quickly to Emma. "Undress and get into bed. You're sick with a pain in your stomach. Keep the bedroom door shut."

I dropped the dirty glasses and empty wine bottle in the garbage pail, went down and opened up the front door. The two men could well have been insurance salesmen. They were sharply dressed and knowing eyed. The one in a blue camelhair topcoat showed me a warrant card in a plastic case. His smile was amiable enough.

"Police officers. Detective Inspector Gagan. This is Detective Sergeant Pappa. Is there a Canadian gentleman living at this address, a Mr. James Hamilton?"

I was leaning with both hands on the wall, blocking their way in. "What's he supposed to have done?"

"Are you Mr. Hamilton?"

I nodded cautiously. There was a third man sitting at the wheel of the police car.

Gagan's smile looked as if he practised hard at it. "This is just a routine inquiry, Mr. Hamilton. About a Mr. Gavin Legge. I understand that you know him?"

At least he still had Legge in the present tense. "I've met the guy a couple of times," I allowed. "But I wouldn't say *know* him."

Sergeant Pappa grunted. My answer

hadn't gone too well with him.

"If you've met him you know him. That's what the Inspector means."

"A purist," apologized Gagan. His affability persisted. "Perhaps we could talk inside?"

"By all means," I said. "Come on upstairs."

I led the way up to the sitting room. The bedroom door was closed.

"Very pleasant," said Gagan, looking round the room. The Sheraton chairs belonged to Emma's family. The fire had just caught, the light catching the pieces of Chinese silk tapestry. He sat on the sofa, his camelhair coat spread across his knees, looking as if he was about to give me a spiel about linked policies, mortgage, life and the like. Pappa chose to stand, assuming a posture like a rugby football halfback waiting for the ball to be snapped from the serum. We give the occasional party and though it's a small room we've had as many as twelve in it without having to sit in each other's laps. But these two men loomed — I can think of no other word — their eyes, ears and noses seemed to be everywhere, under the carpet, inside drawers and on top of the bookcase and all this they managed to achieve without moving a muscle.

Gagan's hair was bog-black and his eyes the blue that goes with it.

"When did you last see Mr. Legge?" he asked casually.

The question took me by surprise. I'd expected it to come by a far more devious route.

"The day before yesterday. Right outside Knightsbridge Crown Courts."

A million and a half readers of the *Globe* must have seen the picture of Legge, Shane and me. Gagan made it sound all very normal.

"That would be after the assault case. By the way, you weren't a defence witness, were you, Mr. Hamilton?"

I had the impression that he knew more about the Legge case than I did. I was beginning to feel like someone trapped in a sinking boat, dashing from side to side and trying to plug the leaking holes.

"No, I wasn't a witness," I replied. "But I was one of Mr. Stafford's sureties. His sister and I live together." I was pretty sure too that this was gratuitous information.

He nodded, glancing across at the framed photograph of Emma. "Congratulations. A very good looking young lady. She puts me in mind of a niece of mine. Is there any Irish in her at all?"

"As far as I know she's one hundred per cent English."

"Well now." He smiled and put the next statement easily, a piece of chat between two friends. "There seems to have been quite a lot of bad feeling between Legge and the Stafford family. Almost a feud, would you say?"

"There *was*," I corrected. "They buried the hatchet yesterday. You must have seen the picture in the *Globe*."

He made a small gesture with plump fingers that could have meant yes or it could have meant no. The only light burning in the sitting room came from the pedestal-lamp. A brighter strip showed at the bottom of the bedroom door.

"Miss Stafford wouldn't be in, I suppose?" Gagan inquired artlessly.

"She's in but she's sick in bed," I said firmly. "As a matter of fact I was just going to call the doctor when you people rang the doorbell."

"I'm sorry about that," he said swiftly and glanced at his watch. "Well, we won't detain you any longer. There's only one more question I'd like to ask you. What you're saying is that you haven't seen Mr. Legge since the day before yesterday, is that it?"

"Correct," I replied. I was suddenly very conscious of the weight of their joint inspection. I could see myself in the mirror by the bookcase, a credit to my drama school, my manner displaying a blend of confidence and innocence. My performance would have been still better had my stomach stayed still. "Look," I added. "Let's get one thing straight, Inspector. I've read the newspapers. I can assure you that I have as much idea where Legge is as you have. Possibly less, come to think of it. Now if you'll excuse me I really must call the doctor."

Gagan came to his feet. "Of course. I'm sorry about all this, Mr. Hamilton. It's as bloody boring for us as it is for you. You'll have to take my word for it. There are seven more people to see before we go off duty tonight."

The taxi-driver's statement that he had seen Legge's car must have set the cat among the pigeons. But there was no suggestion as yet that he had recognized either Shane or me from the photograph in the *Globe*. I could only suppose that he hadn't seen it. There was a sneaking feeling however that it was only a matter of time before the cops started to pull the string tighter.

I opened the door to the stairs. Gagan held out his hand so I shook it. Pappa contented himself with a nod. I offered a tentative smile to let them know that a joke was intended. "Where was I on the list of suspects?"

Gagan answered deadpan. "Number two. Goodnight, Mr. Hamilton."

I watched them from the kitchen window. They both climbed into the police car and drove off without as much as a backward glance. Then the mews was silent again. I drew the curtains. Emma was huddled under the sheets with the electric blanket on. Her hands were cold. I sat down and warmed them.

"Did you hear all that?"

She nodded from the pillow. "Most of it. What are we going to do, Jamie?"

We'd achieved something, anyway. She was asking me now instead of telling me. The bedroom was warm and inviting. What I would like to have done was to get into bed with her and pull the blinds on the last forty-eight hours.

"I suppose the first thing is to get

hold of Shane. Have you any idea where he went?"

Her face was very tired suddenly. "None at all. He said he needed to think things over."

"The understatement of the year," I observed. "I'll have to try to find him. He wouldn't be with Amanda, would he?"

She shook her head. "She lives with her sister and brother-in-law. He couldn't stay there. In any case he wouldn't want to. It's between us all this and nobody else."

She groped for my hand again, her small boyish face pale against the green sheets.

"Do you think the police suspect us, Jamie?"

I tried to keep the resentment out of my voice. "I don't *know* what the hell I think." It was true.

I gripped her fingers. At the moment she needed strength and I was no Rock of Gibraltar. The police had left me with the impression that they'd come looking for more than they'd found. There'd been nothing really heavy in anything they had said or done. On the contrary, their menace lay in the informality of their manner. There was a suggestion that they were biding their time to pounce. Familiar things began to take on a new and sinister light.

I tried to explain and at the same time not scare her too much.

"Listen darling. There's one thing that I *am* sure of. We've been had with this caper of Shane's. We should never have gone into it in the first place. Now we're in trouble. All three of us are in trouble and it's no time to be divided. What we have to do is stick together. Agree on a common policy."

"What common policy?"

"I wish to Christ I knew," I said fervently.

She was lost for the moment, lost and uncertain but I knew from experience that it wouldn't last. The steel inside her spirit might bend but it would never break.

"I'm scared, Jamie," she said again as if reading my thoughts.

I kissed her bruised cheek. "That makes two of us. And if Shane's got any sense at all, he'll be scared too. We just have to accept the fact that those cops may have a whole lot of better cards to play with than they showed us up here. The thing is, they don't know what we know. Not yet, at least. Our best chance is to move before they do."

"You mean run?"

The aeroplane tickets I had bought were on top of the dressing table, the five hundred pounds in the small righthand drawer.

"It's too late for that. What we have to do is come up with some sort of answer that doesn't turn us into killers."

She winced at the word. "Where are you going?"

I slid off the bed. "To try to find Shane. Don't answer the door and keep away from the phone. I'll be back just as soon as I can."

I decided to use public transport on the basis that if the police *were* watching me I'd have more chance to detect it. There was a hint of fog in the mews outside, the freezing fog that creeps under doors and through windows carrying a faint smell of sulphur with it. I walked up the mews with my ears sticking out on stalks, listening for the first hint of following footsteps.

I'd read my suspense stories and peopled the doorways with silent figures in raincoats, imagined each parked car with its duo of cops lying low on their shoulder blades. The only thing I saw was the mews cat asleep on a window ledge. When I reached Sussex Place I broke into a jog, doing my best to look like someone out on a keep-fit exercise.

I kept it up as far as Bayswater Road, pretty sure by then that no one was following me. A bus took me down Park Lane. Visibility was worsening when I dropped off at Knightsbridge. I skirted the back of Harrods and made my way round to the end wall of Shane's garden. The bricks at the top were green and slippery. I climbed up leaving scrapings of skin from my arms and legs. The ground came sooner than I expected, the shock of landing thudding up from my heels to my jawbone. The garden was dark and quiet but a light was shining in Shane's kitchen. I ran across the grass and rattled my knuckles on the back door. A shadow showed behind the blind. Then the kitchen window was raised. I showed myself and Shane lifted a hand. Seconds later I heard the back door being unlocked.

Everything upstairs looked normal. The blinds were down, the fire burning. A felt pen was resting on a copy of the *Evening Standard*. Shane had evidently been solving the crossword puzzle.

He gave me the quick appraising look of the Staffords when they're deciding a course of action.

"Emma told you."

I brushed the green mould from my

trousers and dropped onto the sofa.

"She told me. Look, a couple of cops have just been round to my place asking questions."

He took the news in his stride, amazingly calm and relaxed. "Yes. They've been here too. What did you tell them?"

"Nothing," I said. "How about you?"

He was sprinkling fishfood into the tank. "Me? I'd have thought you'd have known me better than that."

The expression on his face exploded me. "What is it with you, for crissakes! What do you think you've done that's so clever? A man has been killed!"

His eyes grew cold. "I don't need you to tell me what happened. I *know* what I've done."

Apart from hangmen and priests, nobody seems to worry too much about other people's death except when the victims are close. And Legge *was* close. We'd *made* him close. There was something scary about Shane's indifference. A sort of inhumanity that I instinctively challenged.

"A man's dead," I said and held up my hand as he started to interrupt. "No, you listen to *me*! Ok. I'll accept that it was an accident but we can't just walk away as though it never happened. Forget the moral side of it, let's be practical. If that taxi-driver is shown the picture that Legge had taken outside Knightsbridge Crown Court he's going to recognize us as the men he saw in the car that night. Have you thought of that?"

"I've no need to think of it." He had lost none of his brash self-assurance. "It was on the six o'clock news. The B.B.C. interviewed our friend at his home. His description of the people he saw in the car was an absolute cock-up. He said there were three men all in their twenties and the girl driving had long black hair."

I shook my head slowly. It all sounded too pat for me and one doubt after another flitted through my mind.

"How do you know it's not some kind of a trick? Suppose the guy just happens to pick up a copy of that newspaper — somebody gives it to him — and then he remembers?"

He emptied the last of the fishfood into the tank. "Don't worry about it. We're the only ones who really know what's happened to Legge. As long as we keep it that way there's no danger. If the worst comes to the worst we can always confess that we did steal Legge's car. We were going to take it and smash it up. Then one of us had second thoughts and we returned it to the garage. Legge himself we never saw. There's no way they can prove differently."

There was ash on the carpet. I rubbed it in with my foot. "You sound as though you're actually pleased with yourself."

His surprise was genuine. "What do you expect me to do, burst into tears? That bastard destroyed my sister's life and was trying to do the same to mine. Of course I'm pleased that he's no longer with us."

Incredibly enough there wasn't a single word of regret for dragging Emma and me down with him. I shook my head.

"It's not going to work, Shane. A man's dead and we're responsible. I'll tell you what I'm going to do. I'm going to see Patrick Joseph."

He turned on me like a treed bobcat. "You're going to do *what*?"

I said it again. "The thing we need most is proper advice. Patrick Joseph is a friend as well as a lawyer. It's no good you getting heavy about it, Shane. I'm seeing Patrick Joseph whether you like it or not. For Emma's sake as well as my own."

His face narrowed, "What gives you the right to be so bloody high-minded? You may be Emma's lover but I'm her brother. You'll find there's a vast difference, my friend. I'll be around long after you've gone."

All it needed was a threatening

gesture, one more wrong word, and I knew that we'd be at one another's throats. I got to my feet.

"You've got your signals crossed. I'm not going anywhere. I'm staying right here and what's more I'm going to be taking care of Emma. *That*'s the difference."

We stood facing one another, the gulf between us widening every second.

"I'm sorry," he said impulsively. "I'm saying all the stupid things. Look, Jamie, do me one favour. Don't go to Patrick Joseph. I give you my word that it can only make things worse. It isn't necessary."

"What do you want to do then?" I demanded. "Wait until we're sitting in the cells to contact him?"

"No," he said quietly. "I've got a plan."

"So have I," I replied. "I intend to find out just what sort of shit you've landed us in. Whether it's murder or manslaughter."

"*Murder?*" He repeated the word as

though hearing it for the first time in his life.

"That's right," I replied. "Something about death following as the result of a criminal conspiracy. I'm no expert but that sounds pretty much like murder to me." It was worse now that it was out of my head and into my mouth.

"It was an accident," he said flatly.

"An accident?" I ticked off the points on my fingers. "Number one: we abduct Legge at gunpoint. Number two: you threaten to blow off his head. Number three: you fire a gun at him and miss but he comes up dead. We'll need an act of parliament to get us out of this!"

He put his hand on my sleeve. "Don't go to Patrick Joseph, Jamie. There's no need for him to know anything. No need for anyone to know. Leave things the way they are. I've got a plan," he repeated.

A faint hope jumped in my brain. It was possible that they might have been mistaken, that they'd seen a lot of blood and panicked, that Legge was lying injured but still alive.

"How do you know that Legge's dead?"

Shane's glance fell to his hands. I don't know what he saw there but his voice left no room for doubt.

"There was no pulse and no breathing. He's dead all right. His head was split like a melon."

There was nothing more to do or say. I buttoned my jacket. "I'd better get back to Emma. You can let me out through the garden in case the place is being watched."

He grinned from the landing. "You've been reading too many books. If they were going to watch everyone that Legge had trouble with they'd need an entire police force."

The fog was settling outside, shrouding the trees. He unlocked the door at the end of the garden. "Will you give me your word that you won't do anything stupid?"

I looked him in the eye and saw

Emma. "That depends what you mean by stupid."

He hesitated, his outstretched hand still demanding the pledge. "You know what I mean. I'm talking about going to the police or to Patrick Joseph."

"I'll see you tomorrow," I answered. "We all need some sleep. And don't call me at home."

I must have walked the streets for an hour or more, trying to get my head straightened out. It would all have been somehow easier if Shane had shown the slightest concern and understanding for Emma if not for me. The more I thought about things, the clearer my course became. I *had* to know how we stood.

The direction I had taken, maybe unconsciously, had brought me within a quarter of a mile from where Patrick Joseph O'Callaghan lived. I found a booth free at Sloane Square and called his number.

"It's me," I said, "Jamie Hamilton." His voice held no surprise. "How are you, Jamie? What can I do for you?"

"I'd like to see you," I volunteered. "Right away if that's possible."

"Where are you now?"

"Sloane Square Underground Station."

"Then make your way round here." The dialling tone followed.

A bus careered out of the thickening fog, its headlamps staring. I rode it as far as Chelsea Town Hall and walked south towards the river. I'd been to Patrick Joseph's place half-a-dozen times, mostly to parties. He likes inviting people of dissimilar tastes and ages, what he calls casting against type. I've met a jazz pianist, a transvestite County Court judge and a mountain climber all on the same evening. The mountain climber was a woman. His gatherings seem to work maybe because he has the gift of putting everyone at ease.

He lives in an old-fashioned block between Kings Road and the Embankment, a building that straddles two streets with a courtyard in between.

There were fresh flowers in the lobby. The brass was highly polished and there was an atmosphere of absolute respectability.

He answered his doorbell immediately, greeting me as if he hadn't clapped eyes on me for months. A wayward plume of hair nodded at the back of his head.

"How nice to see you, Jamie."

He was dressed in a maroon-coloured smoking-jacket, black velvet trousers and jet-beaded evening slippers.

It was, as they say, another world. The back of his front door was lined with bookshelves so that closed the door vanishes. The effect is slightly claustrophobic. A selection of his capes was hanging in the hall, like birds of prey with their wings folded. *Trompe l'oeil* on one of the walls created a vista of tropical plants and insects seen through parted black curtains. He had been listening to Chopin. The headphones were on the table, the record still playing. He offered me a seat, indicating the bottle of *Pernod* on the opium table.

"Or perhaps you'd prefer something else?"

There were six of the scarlet-upholstered chairs, bought from a firm of ecclesiastical furnishers. There was a cigar burning in the ashtray next to the *Pernod*. Patrick Joseph allows himself two a day except on Sundays when he fasts.

"Scotch, please," I answered and sat.

"What's it like outside?" His dark blue eyes were bright and interested. He's *always* interested. It's part of his charm.

"Thickening all the time," I said, swirling the whisky and water.

He sat down, threw his head back and blew a series of smoke-rings. I've pulled him out of a snowbank he skied into by mistake, I've heard a drunken woman accuse him of latent homosexuality but I've never seen Patrick Joseph lose his presence.

There was a pile of old theatre programmes on the floor beside me. Collecting them is one of his hobbies.

"I need your advice about a couple of things," I said, knowing that I was going to lie and feeling bad about it.

He closed an eye, avoiding the stream of cigar smoke. "Fire away."

He must have sensed my uncertainty because he opened both eyes and smiled.

"I can guess what it is. You want to talk about Legge, right?"

"That's one of the things," I agreed. "What do you make of this vanishing trick?"

He added water to the green liquid in his glass and the mixture turned cloudy. He dropped in three lumps of ice, one after another and very slowly.

"I don't know that I've formed an opinion as yet. The trouble is with a clown like Legge there are all sorts of possibilities. The first thing that comes to mind is that it's some sort of publicity stunt."

"The police came to see me this evening," I said bluntly. "Asking questions about him."

He flipped the record on the player. "I imagined they might as soon as I read the news. It was almost predictable in the circumstances. Did they go to see Shane or don't you know?"

It was pointless to lie. "They did. I'm not too sure what they said to him but they wanted to know the last time I'd seen Legge. I told them the truth — outside Knightsbridge Crown Courts. There were two of them."

He nodded. "Detective Inspector Gagan and Detective Sergeant Pappa."

I put my glass down deliberately. "Now how in hell could you know that, Patrick Joseph?"

He put his fingers to the side of his head. "Extrasensory perception." Then he smiled. "I saw it on television. The hunt for the missing journalist headed by officers Gagan and Pappa. The next instalment is at nine o'clock in fact. In exactly eleven minutes' time." He

161

glanced at the elegant clock over the fireplace.

"What else did they say?" My attempt to make my voice sound casual was pathetic.

He blew a couple more rings. "Nothing much, really. The taxi-driver was interviewed and a couple of Legge's ex-girl friends. Were the police civil or did they give you a hard time?"

"It was cool," I replied. "The way cops are supposed to behave. You know, the one who's supposed to be your friend and the heavy. They only stayed about a quarter of an hour. They asked to see Emma but she was in bed with a stomach ache."

He considered the end of his cigar. "I think you'd better give me a buzz if they do come back, Jamie. I'm sure it's only a formality but I'd like to be there nevertheless. Just say that you're not prepared to make any statement at all unless your solicitor is present. They can stop me being there in the police station but not in your home."

He crossed his elegant ankles and closed his eyes, listening to the music. It has always seemed strange to me that he dresses up to cook his generally solitary meals. His girl friends never seem to last too long. Maybe it's because none of them compete with his passion for the law.

"Do you think that they will come back?" I didn't like the idea of it one little bit.

He waved a hand. "It's a possibility. On the other hand, Legge may well turn up at any moment with yet another of his so-called exposures."

I decided to change the subject. "I wanted to see you about something else. It's for a friend, a writer of suspense stories with a problem. I said that you'd help."

He gave the sweet smile that you sometimes see on the faces of blind people.

"I will if I can, of course."

It was difficult to sound convincing and I knew it would be dangerous to flounder. He's not only smart, he's sensitive.

"He's created this character who helps spring a friend from the slammer. A guard is accidentally killed in the getaway. I mean the guard falls from the wall. He's not shot or anything. What my friend wants to know, is his guy guilty of murder or not?"

Paderewski's playing sweetened the ensuing silence. "It's a difficult one to answer," he said at length. "At least without knowing more details."

I knew exactly what he meant but I dared not give him too much information in case he began to wonder.

"That's what I thought," I said. "He'd heard from somebody who's supposed to know that a death resulting from a criminal conspiracy is murder, whether accidental or not."

He shoved his fingers through his wild hair. "Off hand I'd say that intent would be the major factor. But it would also depend on circumstances.

I'm sorry I can't be of more help, Jamie. Maybe your friend would care to let me see a draft or something."

"I'll tell him," I said.

He fixed another drink for us and turned on the television. It was two minutes to nine. A woman with a Valkyrie hairstyle and wearing several rows of beads announced the latest rounds of what she called 'industrial action'. She touched on the state of the pound and fixed the camera intimately.

"The disappearance of Gavin Legge. New developments in the case of the missing gossip-columnist include alleged sightings of the missing journalist in Gastaad, Nassau and Venice, all of which places Mr. Legge is known to be familiar with. Interpol has been alerted. Meanwhile a Scotland Yard spokesman stated tonight that the police have not ruled out the possibility of an accident or foul play. Forensic experts are making a further examination of the journalist's car and Mr. Mark Krantz is to be shown a number of photographs tomorrow morning. Mr. Krantz lives in Hoxton and is the taxi-driver who claims to have seen the journalist's car on the night of his disappearance. The A24 controversy . . ."

Patrick Joseph switched the set off. His bow tie was askew and ash streaked his lapels.

"The Beeb really loves its clichés, doesn't it? 'A Scotland Yard spokesman' forsooth! Old Jack Fogarty in the pressroom, as drunk as a skunk twelve hours a day."

I tried to raise a smile to match his and failed. I felt as though I'd been kicked in the stomach yet one more time. Showing the taxi-driver photographs could mean only one thing. The pictures the police would produce would be of people they suspected might have something to do with Legge's disappearance. I knew that Shane and I were on that list and I knew that the only pictures they could have of us was the one taken outside the courts. I remembered the way Gagan had looked at Emma's photograph, the sound of his voice. "A good-looking young lady."

Patrick Joseph was changing the record. "The whole thing stinks of a put-up job. I'd be willing to bet that it's some kind of stunt that Legge organized."

My mind was still with Krantz and the police. He substituted Bach for Chopin and continued from his chair.

"You'll see. He'll turn up in a couple of days with the scandal of the year."

I was picturing a spreadeagled body with its head smashed in, lying seventy-five feet underground. Coming here had made no real sense. It was no more than what my grandfather had called 'the cancer of indecision' that had plagued me for years. I needed Patrick Joseph's advice, but I couldn't bring myself to tell him the truth. I collected my cigarettes and lighter.

"You're probably right. Thanks a lot, Patrick Joseph."

He came to his feet, warm and

hospitable. "You're not going, are you? Come on now, let me get you something to eat."

"No, I'd better get back," I replied. "Emma's on her own."

"Of course," he said quickly. "Give her my love."

He came to the hallway with me. "About Shane," I said impulsively.

His eyes were suddenly wary. "What about him, Jamie?"

I was at the tip of my tongue away from telling him everything, of laying the whole mess in his lap. It was the thought of Emma that held me back. She would never forgive me. I shrugged.

"Emma worries a lot about him."

He fended that one off with ease. "The Staffords have always worried about one another. It was the same when the parents were alive. Have you two ever thought of having a child?"

He caught me flatfooted. It was about the last thing I expected him to say.

"Why do you ask?"

His breath was redolent of *Pernod* and cigar smoke. "It would give her a fresh interest. Shane's big enough to stand on his own feet. Looking after him is a lost cause anyway. He doesn't play by other people's rules."

I gave him my hand. "Goodnight, Patrick Joseph and thanks again. It was good talking with you."

He opened the door. "Don't forget now, if the police do come back, refuse to talk to them unless I'm present. I'll be in court all day tomorrow and the next day but my secretary will know how to get hold of me."

He let me out facing an elderly woman holding a ginger-coloured Chow. She must have heard Patrick Joseph's farewell remarks and stared disapprovingly at my sneakers and jeans as I sidled past her dog.

Outside, the fog was clinging to everything, making watery yellow globes of the streetlamps. Some sounds seemed sharper and clearer, the tap of heels on the sidewalks, the crunch of metal as a bus-driver shifted gears. Passers-by covered their mouths with scarves or gloved hands as if in fear of the plague. The chance of finding a cab was slim. My best bet was the Underground and I walked as far as Sloane Square. I was home by a quarter to ten. The fog was too thick for me to see the houses at the other end of the mews. I started to put the car away. The cat was asleep on the radiator. The motor was stone-cold but habit dies hard. I hit the starting-button and the cat jumped, stretching one leg after another after landing and stalking away stiff-tailed.

Emma was still in bed, sitting up wearing one of my sweaters. She hadn't bothered to put more coal on the fire but she'd eaten. I could see the remains on the kitchen table. She was also back on the wine. A bottle was on the bedside table near her. I bent down and kissed her.

"Why were you so long?" she complained.

I'd had no supper but I wasn't hungry. I skipped my bath and got in beside her. I closed my eyes for a moment.

"I asked you why you were so long?" she asked tugging my hair.

"There were things to do," I protested.

"Like what?" I didn't answer and felt her lift on an elbow. "Did you find Shane?"

I opened my eyes. "There's egg on your chin. I saw him, yes."

"What happened with the police? What did they say to him?"

I reached across her for a cigarette. Normally I never smoke in bed but then there were a whole lot of things I was doing that I didn't do normally. Smoking in bed was the least of them.

"He wasn't exactly expansive," I said. "But he certainly didn't seem worried. He made that plain. You see, he's got this plan."

She picked up on it straight away.

171

"What's the sarcasm for? You haven't been quarrelling with Shane again, have you?"

The implication was that trouble if any would come from me and I resented it. I shifted my head towards her.

"I don't like the way your brother's behaving. It isn't normal."

A violet vein in her neck starts to throb when she's under stress. Or maybe it was the wine. "He's scared," she said. "That's why. None of us are acting normally."

I made a sound of disbelief. "Bullshit! You may be scared. I'm certainly scared but not Shane. Hell, no! He's got the whole thing under control. You wanted to know where I was tonight. Ok, I'll tell you. I was walking the streets trying to think of some way to get ourselves out of the shit we're in. And I thought that Patrick Joseph O'Callaghan could help. I went to see him."

She caught her breath quickly. "Oh no! You're kidding!"

"I'm not kidding," I told her.

She put her glass on the table beside her. *"You told Patrick Joseph O'Callaghan about kidnapping Legge? That he's dead?"*

"I told him nothing," I said firmly. "But I wouldn't want to bet that he doesn't already smell something."

"You mean he suspects us?" The thought brought her bolt upright in the bed. "Why should he?"

I toyed with the hair hanging over my face. It smelled of her body.

"It's an impression I get. Patrick Joseph's no fool and he's a lot closer to us than the police are. He knows how you two feel about Legge for instance."

She shook her head, freeing her hair from my fingers. "I don't believe it. He's known us for fifteen years. He'd have said something."

"Wrong," I corrected. "It's because he's known you for fifteen years that he *wouldn't* say anything. He probably doesn't want to know."

She screwed up her face, stretching the band of freckles across her nose.

"Why did you go to see Patrick Joseph in the first place?"

I tried to explain. "Shane seems to think that what's happened is no more than some kind of practical joke that's gone sour on him. Well I don't go for it. What I think is that we're in a whole slew of trouble and I wanted to know the truth. *That*'s why I went to see Patrick Joseph."

She locked her hands behind her head, suddenly very controlled. "And what did you find out?"

I ground the end of my cigarette into the ashtray. "Nothing. You have to put truthful questions to get truthful answers. I lost my nerve and talked a lot of crap about some friend who was supposed to be a writer with a plot problem to do with an accidental killing. Patrick Joseph said I hadn't told him enough to go on, that he couldn't give proper advice without knowing a lot more about the circumstances. He

174

gave me the chance to talk but I just couldn't take it."

She looked at me hard. "What you *really* want to do, Jamie, is go to the police, isn't it? To make a confession and ask for your bloody absolution."

"I guess so," I admitted finally. "I'm out of my depth and I accept it. But it's not just myself that concerns me."

"So what have you decided to do?" Her eyes searched mine for the answer.

"Nothing." It was difficult to keep the bitterness out of my voice. "Shane got us into this mess. I guess we have to give him the chance to get us out of it. That's what *you* want, isn't it?"

She touched my shoulder with soft gentle fingers and smiled. "I really do love you, Jamie. Because above all, you understand."

It was untrue but I liked to hear it. "They're showing pictures to the driver tomorrow. I heard it on the news at Patrick Joseph's. If they show him pictures of us it's going to be our word against his. Shane's idea is that we admit taking Legge's car."

Her expression was puzzled. "Admit stealing his car? But why?"

I explained. "We're going to say that our intention was to crash it, to teach Legge a lesson. Then one of us got scared and we put it back in the garage where we found it. Legge we never saw. This is just if the worst should come to the worst, remember."

I switched off the light. Her voice sounded beside me in the darkness.

"I don't think that's a good idea. Do *you* think that's a good idea?"

"I think it stinks," I replied. "But short of telling the truth I can't think of a better one."

"Do you think the police could find out about the tobacconist's shop?"

The thought had never left the back of my mind. The board hanging outside the empty premises with Shane's name and address on it. "Shane's probably done something about it — hidden the file on the property. I'll ask him tomorrow."

Our bodies came close. There was nowhere else for them to go.

I woke with a cold grey light at the window, reminding me that I hadn't closed the curtains the night before. I groped my way into the bathroom, found my robe and went into the kitchen. The mews was filled with fog, making an island of each house. I let Emma sleep on. Nothing had changed overnight. There was one of Gagan's cigarette ends in the sitting room ashtray. I switched on the kitchen radio, plugged in the kettle and toaster and stuck a couple of yoghurts on the breakfast tray. The first thing we had to do was get hold of Shane. I'd slept fitfully, wondering about his 'plan'. Nothing would be too crazy for him. I wanted to go back to Highgate to see Legge's body and make certain it all wasn't part of some ghastly nightmare. In a perverse sort of way I wanted to reassure myself of the worst.

I heard the mail hit the mat and went downstairs. The papers had already been delivered. I picked them up from the floor and started reading the *Globe*. Legge's column was still going out under his byline. The morning's banner was:

X DAY PLUS TWO

The entire piece was devoted to Legge's life and works. The writer claimed that beneath Legge's abrasive exterior was a heart of gold, a fine sensitivity that included such gestures as contributing books to prison libraries and playing cricket in aid of the cancer fund. The readers were reminded that Legge was the champion of the underdog. There were no inspired guesses as to what might have happened to him. I was halfway up the stairs when I heard the radio announcer's voice coming from the kitchen.

"This is L.B.C. where news comes to you every hour on the hour, Keith Howell reporting! First the Gavin Legge syndrome. Mr. Mark

Krantz, forty years of age and a London taxi-driver was found dead in his garage in the early hours of the morning. Mr. Krantz was a key witness in the case of the missing journalist that has been intriguing his public for the last couple of days. Mr. Krantz had been helping police with their inquiries into the missing reporter's movements on Thursday and was due to attend a meeting at Scotland Yard this morning. The dead man's body was found by his brother-in-law, Mr. Bernard Siegel who lives next door. Mr. Siegel described how he heard the taxi return shortly after midnight. Mr. Krantz had been working the late shift all week. Twenty minutes passed by and the motor of the taxi was still running so Mr. Siegel decided to investigate. He found the garage closed and full of carbon-monoxide and the dead man lying there with his head close to the exhaust pipe. Resuscitation was tried but to no avail. First reports indicate that Mr. Krantz had left his vehicle, omitting to switch off the engine. It is thought that he closed the garage doors, stumbled and fell on his way back, hitting his head in the process. A coroner's inquest opens tomorrow."

I listened to the rest of the news without taking any of it in. I carried the breakfast tray into the bedroom, closed the curtains and switched on the lights. Emma stirred, shading her eyes and grumbling. I lifted her up and draped her robe round her shoulders. I put the tray in her lap. She was still half asleep and I waited till she had gulped some tea before speaking.

"Krantz is dead. The taxi-driver. He was found in his garage early this morning, asphyxiated. I just heard it on the radio."

She nibbled a piece of toast, a lock of red hair falling over her lazy eyes.

"Did you hear what I said?" I demanded.

She nodded. "I heard. So much the better."

"I don't believe it!" I said. "I'm

telling you that a man is dead!"

She put the tray on the table beside her. I noticed that her fingers were far from steady.

"What exactly do you expect me to say, Jamie?"

I sat on the edge of the bed. "That was no accident."

She looked at me coolly. "How the hell would you know whether it was or wasn't?"

She was making me do it the hard way. "*Shane* killed him," I said deliberately.

She tried to laugh, colour flaring in her throat and face. "You are incredible! Shane killed him? I thought you just said that he was found asphyxiated."

"I did," I answered. "He was found asphyxiated after Shane laid him out." The details were cloudy but I knew I was right.

She pushed the suggestion aside. "It's not true. He couldn't and wouldn't."

"Bullshit!" I answered. "He could

and he did. He's sick in the head, that's why. And the sooner both of you realize it the better!"

She swung at the side of my head but I managed to catch her wrist.

"Don't do it," I warned. "I never hit a woman in my life and I wouldn't want you to be first."

She answered by swinging her other arm. I rolled onto the bed, smothering her flailing limbs till I finally straddled her, pinning her down with my knees on her shoulders. Blood was running down my cheek where her fingernail had raked me. We were both breathing heavily and her eyes were savage.

"Ok," I gasped. "You can get your clothes on. You and I are going to pay your brother a visit."

For one horrible moment I thought she was going to spit in my face. Her voice was as taut as a harp string.

"Will you please let me get up?"

I climbed off her, soaked a piece of cotton in cologne and dabbed it on my face. I eyed her warily but she paid me no attention, slipping into her robe and carrying the breakfast things through to the kitchen. I heard the crashing of plates in the sink, she changed the radio station. The bleeding had stopped on my face leaving a slight scratch a couple of inches long. I shaved round it, dressed and prepared a new fire. By now Emma was in the bathroom. We weren't speaking.

Yesterday's newspapers were on the kitchen table, ready to be taken downstairs with the ashes. The dead driver's picture stared up at me over the caption.

LONDON TAXI-DRIVER SPOTS
MISSING JOURNALIST'S CAR!
(Mr. Mark Krantz,
256 Hackney Way, E6. See p. 12)

I wrapped the ashes in the papers and took them down to the dustbin in the mews. Krantz's death had shaken me rigid. There was no doubt in my mind that he had been murdered, no doubt that Emma's brother was the killer. Something had happened to him since the trial or maybe I was seeing him as he was for the first time. I had often thought that there was something flawed or twisted in the twins' make-up that Emma had been spared.

It all added up. Shane would have known the driver's home address and he certainly *had* the motive. Part of his confidence must have stemmed from the fact that the police couldn't know that he had a motive. When I went upstairs, Emma was in the sitting room manicuring her nails. She'd scraped her hair back and tied it with a ribbon and was wearing a shabby old loden cloth coat over jeans. If there'd been a prize for making the worst of herself she'd have won it. She spoke for the first time in half-an-hour.

"You realize of course that nothing will ever be the same again between us after this."

"Oh great!" I said. The coldness in her voice was hard to take. "I'm trying to save you from being destroyed and you want to take my head off! What's *happening* to us, Emma? I love you, for crissakes. Or don't you realize that?"

I took her in my arms but it was like holding a bale of hay. She disengaged herself deliberately, her small face hard and determined.

"I always suspected that you had a down on Shane, some sort of jealous feeling. Now I'm sure of it. Your friendship for him is just a big act."

It had happened to me before. You look at someone you know and trust and suddenly you see a stranger. I couldn't accept that this was happening to Emma and me. The truth was that she loved her brother blindly, no matter what, and I was the one to show understanding.

"Let's move it," I said quietly.

The fog outside cancelled any form of transport other than the Underground. We surfaced at Knightsbridge. The watery lights in Harrods windows made patterns like moire silk. Disembodied street lamps helped us to Lennox Gardens. It was difficult to see the houses on the other side of the road. I rang Shane's doorbell without getting an answer. I put my ear to the flap on the mailbox. I heard nothing. No lights were burning in the house that I could see.

"It's Saturday," I said over my shoulder. "Amanda won't be here."

There was something secret in Emma's eyes as she watched me from a lower step, a hint of mockery as if she knew something that I didn't.

"Wait here," I told her and hurried round the corner to the gardens in back. I took off from somebody's garbage can, negotiated the wall and landed on frost-stiffened grass. I tossed a handful of dirt at Shane's kitchen window but nothing happened. There was a pile of old newspapers by the back door. I wrapped a half-brick in one of them and put it through an office window. Then I stuck my arm through carefully, avoiding the jagged splinters, and released the catch. I climbed through and unfastened the street door. Emma was quickly in and I closed the door behind her. Shane's apartment was locked. Emma spoke from the hallway.

"Amanda has a key that she keeps in her desk."

I found it among a collection of rubber-bands, old lipsticks and some clippings about Shane's trial. We let ourselves into the second floor flat. There was an odd feeling inside though I couldn't put my finger on anything specific. The windows were shut, the fish swimming around in their tank. I hung in the doorway leading to Shane's sleeping quarters, seeing the cane-headed bed and navy blue sheets.

I called to Emma. "Come here a minute."

She peered round my shoulder, her face puzzled. "What am I supposed to be looking at?"

"The dressing table."

Shane's ivory backed hair brushes

flanked a bottle of *Signorricci*. The picture of his twin sister was missing.

"Sara's picture's gone," I said. "He didn't sleep here last night. I doubt if he even came home."

I was certain that I was right. A firm of contract-cleaners attend to Shane's office and apartment on five days a week. They wouldn't have been today since it was Saturday and Shane had never made his own bed in his life. His pyjamas and robe were neatly folded at the foot of it.

"Where does he keep his car-keys?"

She indicated the bedside table. "Then they're gone too," I said.

She was holding a dressing table drawer open. "And his passport."

Both of us jumped as the phone shrilled by the bedside. I grabbed her arm, whispering as if the caller could hear me.

"Don't answer!"

The ringing stopped as abruptly as it had started. I sat down on the sofa and lighted a cigarette. The scratch on my cheek smarted as I inhaled.

"Ok, what have we got here? Shane was supposed to see me this morning. He didn't call and he's certainly not here. Plus the facts that his passport's missing, so's Sara's picture and he's taken his car. Where has he gone and why?"

She wouldn't answer but kept moving around the room, picking things up and putting them down again. She finally did what I was waiting for her to do, opened the bureau drawer where her brother kept his gun. She closed it again but the deadpan expression she wore didn't fool me. I didn't have to look to know that the gun too was missing. I was in the kitchen getting a glass of juice from the icebox when the phone rang a second time. By the time I reached her, Emma already had the instrument in her hand and was speaking.

"Six-two-o-three."

Her neck flamed and the next second drained of all colour. "No, he's not,

I'm afraid." Her voice stumbled on. "I really have no idea. Yes of course I'll see that he gets the message."

She looked at me as though she had just been in touch with the dead. "Detective Inspector Gagan. He wants Shane to get in touch with him at the police station."

She was cranking herself up to preserve the image of the cool confident chick who knows where she's going. But I lived with her. I could see the butterflies in her stomach. No matter how much she enraged me I loved her and I tried to ease her mind.

"It's nothing to be spooked about. If the police really want you they don't send out invitations. They come and get you. What we have to do is find Shane as soon as we can. Have you any idea at all where he'd be? *Think!*"

Our eyes touched. Seventy-five feet below ground with the rats was no place for a man with two deaths on his conscience. Not the way I saw it.

"He won't be there," I assured her.

She nibbled her lip, holding the flat of one hand over an ear. Her bruised cheekbone was still troubling her.

Her face was suddenly bright with discovery. "I know where he might be. Near Cheltenham. Woodmancote. It's a house that belongs to a woman he knows. He goes there at weekends with Amanda. I know the place."

I landed on the suggestion hard. "Who is this woman?"

Emma's tone took on confidence. "Someone called Lucy Sergeant. She spends the winters in Nassau and Shane has the keys. He's meant to keep an eye on the place."

"Do you think you could find the house?" I asked.

She nodded quickly, sure of herself. "I've been there with them on three occasions. The village is eight miles from Cheltenham. The house is called Churchend."

I stuffed the keys to the flat in my pocket. There was a front door key on the ring. We might need to return. It would be Monday before the broken windows were discovered.

"Let's go," I said.

We called Directory Inquiries from Knightsbridge station. The operator gave me the number of the Sergeant woman's house and it started to ring. I passed the receiver to Emma.

Her eyes widened. "What do you want me to say?"

Words collided in my mind. "Just ask him about the driver."

Her gaze flickered and broke. "I can't."

I could hear Shane's voice, thin in the earpiece, then Emma spoke.

"I wanted to ask you . . . " she broke off and listened instead of speaking. When she talked again her voice had completely changed. "Of course I will, darling. Don't worry. I'll *be* there."

Green eyes stared at me from the troubled face. "He wants me to go there immediately."

"Does he know that you're with me?"

She shook her head. "He told me to come alone."

"You're going nowhere alone," I asserted. "From here on in I'm not letting you out of my sight. We go together."

The argument I expected, the bitter denunciation, never came. For some reason she was strangely submissive, holding my arm as we walked down the steps to the trains.

I opened our street door and the fog crept in after us. The house was cold and grey. Everything added to my sense of discouragement. Emma was in the bedroom changing the sheets. I called to her from the sitting room.

"How does he expect you to get there or didn't he say?"

"A train," she answered. "And a taxi from the station."

"Then he's really out of his head," I said. "Did he say what he wants you for?"

She spoke from the doorway, her arms filled with sheets and pillow cases.

"He needs me," she said distinctly.

It was after half past ten, but the room was still dark. "We'll be lucky to get five miles in this," I said. "And I'm not so sure that the trains will be running."

Green eyes held mine for a second then dropped. "You'll manage. You always do."

I went to the kitchen window. London fog always gives me a feeling of claustrophobia, unlike the mists off the lakes at home. Fog is a villain at your throat, choking the life out of you. Only the year before I'd been caught in the tunnel that runs from South Kensington Underground Station to Exhibition Road. It was early in the afternoon with a peasouper thick in the streets outside. I'd gone halfway down the tunnel when I noticed the band of assorted hoodlums waiting for me. There were four of them, skinheads with nail-studded boots. Apart from them and me the subterranean passage was deserted. At that particular moment it looked about fifty miles long. The leader of the gang was a rat-faced fink with rotten teeth and a safety-pin stuck through the lobe of his left ear.

"Let's have it then, mate," he ordered, pulling a cutthroat razor from his belted sweater. "All you got in your pockets and I'll take the watch too."

I went through the motions of opening my jacket. He was sufficiently sure of himself to come the one yard it took for me to plant my foot hard and high in his testicles. I was off and running as he dropped, the sound of his screams and the footsteps of the rest of the gang following me. It wasn't until I reached the end of the tunnel that I realized that we'd been travelling in opposite directions. I took my story to Chelsea police station. The sergeant on desk duty laughed, a good old boy full of beer and street wisdom.

"You have to watch yourself in a Lunnon fog. Stay on the beaten track, don't pick up no women and don't go down the tunnels."

I called the Automobile Association. Traffic on the M4 was reported to be moving at snail's pace with tailbacks up to three miles long. I hung up and called Paddington Station. The switchboard was swamped.

Emma had finished making the bed. She'd brushed her hair but she'd put on no make-up nor had she changed her clothes. She made coffee, slamming my cup down in front of me without a word. Her mood had changed yet again, almost as if she were ashamed of having shown tenderness. I tried to keep my cool. If I'd had my way, we'd both been round at O'Callaghan's office, making a full, complete confession, doing our best to extricate ourselves from the chute we found ourselves in.

I was still standing close to the phone and jumped when it rang again. I lifted the receiver vaguely expecting to hear the voice of British Rail. It was Detective Inspector Gagan speaking with the formal courtesy of an undertaker.

"Mr. Hamilton? I *thought* I recognized the voice. Look, I've been trying to get hold of you since early this morning."

There was an implication that I was somehow at fault by not being there.

"What for?" I asked. I used as few words as possible, memory reminding me that they took them down and used them as evidence.

He replaced the graveyard formality with a kind of jauntiness. "Just a few more routine questions. As a matter of fact I could come to your place now if you like. We're only just around the corner."

I didn't like the implications of that one at all. "No," I said firmly. "Incidentally I've been advised not to see you any more except in the presence of my lawyer."

The line was muffled as he covered the mouthpiece and spoke to a third party. Detective-Sergeant Pappa, no doubt. Gagan was back again playing yet another role. This time he was the dealer from whom you'd gladly buy a used car.

"Come on now, Mr. Hamilton," he said jovially. "There's no need for that. No need to bother Mr. O'Callaghan. I take it that it *is* Mr. O'Callaghan?"

"I don't think that's any of your business," I answered.

He chuckled indulgently. "That's what a lot of people have said. Most of the time it turns out that they're wrong."

Emma had come to the bedroom door. "Not in my case," I said.

He let go with another ho-ho-ho. "My duty is my business. That's the whole point of it, Mr Hamilton."

His manner finally sent me over the top. "Look, Inspector. You make your point by all means but just don't harangue me!"

The one-note hum told me that he'd hung up. My hands were shaking, my adrenalin glands exhausted. Emma was still posing in the doorway. Resentment and anger burst from me.

"What the hell do you and your brother think this is, some kind of parlour game? That was the police, goddammit. They're breathing down our necks."

She kept her composure. "If they want you they come and get you. Isn't that what you said?"

I shook my head sadly. My whole world had come adrift and I needed a point of anchorage. Maybe more than she did, much, much more.

"Emma," I pleaded. "You've got to tell me how we stand. I'm talking about you and your brother and me. I just can't go on playing second fiddle to the guy. Surely you can see that!"

She seemed to glide towards me, bringing her knees up and hovering for the briefest of moments then out with pointed toes.

"I love you, Jamie, but I love Shane too. I've no intention of letting him down."

I took her in my arms. "Nobody's

asking you to let him down. Look, maybe I'm wrong. Maybe the taxi-driver's death *is* a coincidence. It could have been an accident. All I'm asking is that we sit down, the three of us, and talk this thing over without being at one another's throats. If we can do that then we've got some sort of chance."

I didn't believe a word of it but we had to have some sort of working formula. She meditated for a moment then spun the answer at me.

"We've done no more than lots of other people wanted to do. What happened to Legge was unfortunate but you can't blame Shane for it. You can't blame anyone, Jamie."

"Try telling that to Gagan," I said, knowing I was fighting a losing battle.

She smiled. "Why do you have to exaggerate everything?"

It was like talking about Confucius to a pig farmer. I gave up. I'd no idea how we were going to get to Cheltenham. All that came to mind was a picture of a line of cars crawling down the

M4, front-end to rear, other vehicles crashed and abandoned. We had as much hope of covering the hundred and twenty miles as taking off for Mars. I *knew* in my bones that every minute wasted brought us closer to the ultimate disaster that Emma believed was non-existent. Then suddenly the answer clamoured in my head.

"Gordy Grant!" I said out loud.

Emma dropped a mask over her face. She knew exactly who I meant but the name was bad news. I hurried through the pages of my address book. I was taking no chances with this call and walked round the corner to the call boxes on Sussex Street. Gordy answered, his voice thick with sleep.

"Who the hell *is* this?"

I told him. "Look, Gordy, I have to get to Cheltenham and there are no trains. The roads are impossible."

"Then you've got problems," he replied.

"I *have* to get there," I insisted, emphasizing the word.

He yawned. "How's life in the upper echelons?"

It was a reminder that we hadn't talked in months. Emma and Gordy have always disliked one another. He thinks she's snooty while she claims he's a lecher. They're both wrong.

"You know how it goes," I said. "I need your help, Gordy."

"You must be joking," he said loftily. "I'm still in bed. If you were here you'd see the reason why."

I heard a girl laugh. I looked at the gloom outside and thought of Gagan sitting in the police station waiting for me to turn up.

"This is no joke," I said. "You've got to pull one out for me, Gordy."

I thought of the five hundred quid I'd taken out of the bank. The emergency fund. If ever there was an emergency this was it.

"Are you listening?" I asked.

"I'm listening," he said. "But I'm not so goddam sure that I like what I hear."

"I'll charter from you," I urged. "Look, I'll pay the going price and there's a hundred on top for you."

I heard him sigh deeply and the phone was open for a while before he went on.

"Jamie, friend. Air traffic is grounded, dasher! You couldn't fly a kite in what I'm looking at outside my bedroom window. Read a good book and forget Cheltenham."

"Bullshit!" I answered. "You could go up with your head in a bucket. Will you please listen to me, Gordy?"

"What's on your mind?" he asked in a tired voice. "Better still, don't tell me."

"Ok," I said. "I didn't want to have to put it this way but you owe me one."

There was another pause and he sighed again. "It's the story of my life."

It went back a long time, twenty-odd years when we'd both been pupils at Colonel MacTaggart's Mid-Canada

College, a pinebuilt establishment run on the lines of a reformatory, eighty miles north of Thunder Bay. "The *pree*cise *gee*ographical centre of Canada, gentlemen," as the Colonel was given to reminding us. It was a place of spartan education for the sons of gentlefolk in whom the seeds of rebellion had been detected. Here they were instructed in matters of discipline and academic learning. The curriculum was strong on purity of mind and muscular Christianity. Boughs would crack in the silent woods, feathering snow down over a hundred miserable youths who stood naked for five minutes every morning with the thermometer registering fifteen degrees below zero. Colonel MacTaggart used to lead the exercises himself, standing as naked as we were, blue-balled and frosty-bearded, and facing us. The only thing that saved us from death by exposure was the absence of wind and the vigour of our antics. Our free periods were in the evenings between seven and nine.

In summer we walked, swam in the always chilly lake or rode horseback followed by clouds of mosquitos. In winter there was nothing to do but read or play chess with the steam pipes clanking mysteriously throughout the buildings. There was no television. MacTaggart dismissed it as an insult to both God and man along with the Nicene Creed.

Gordy Grant and I had formed an alliance born of still burgeoning seeds of rebellion. As seniors we'd roomed together and played defence on the hockey team. School ended, we kept in touch as the years went by. I heard of him as the boy-wonder of Air Canada, the prestige pilot with his pictures in all the glossy brochures then suddenly nothing. Nobody seemed to know what had happened to him and his family didn't answer my letters. He turned up in England about a year after I did, found me through Canada House and told me a tale of having been in the slammer in India, something to do with running gold from Dubai to Bombay. He needed help. I happened to know a guy running a company called *Winners Helicopter Services*. They ferried jockeys to and from the track. He needed a pilot and Gordy got the job.

I put it to him straight. "It's the big one, Gordy, and I need you."

"Ok," he said jauntily. I guess his mind had been made up from the start. "Ok, you've got me. I can only take two, remember."

"That's all I need, just Emma and me. We'll be there as soon as we can."

I went into the bedroom and stuck the money and passports in my anorak pocket and glanced at Emma. She was sitting on the side of the bed, swinging her legs.

"We're in business. Gordy Grant's going to take us by helicopter."

She hunched a shoulder, turning the ends of her mouth down. She's an odd lady in many ways. She accepted my new friends without question but the old ones seem to represent a challenge that she always refuses to meet. In fact she prefers to ignore their existence, affecting to forget their names and their place in my life.

"Ah well," she said, showing me her profile. "I suppose I'd better call Shane and tell him what's happening."

I put myself between her and the phone. "You're calling nobody. We're doing exactly what he asked us to do and that's all there is to it."

"Not true," she answered. "He doesn't want you there."

"Too bad," I said. "He gets you, he gets me."

She slipped from the bed, her flaming hair stuffed in the green woollen cap, her small face serious.

"I love you, Jamie," she warned. "But don't push too hard."

I opened the door to the stairs, wishing that I could turn the clock back. The word 'love' between us was no more than a springboard for displays of hostility. Deep down was my fear that the love Emma had for her brother would prove to be stronger than the love she had for me.

She bridged the gap at the foot of the stairs, stepping close enough for me to feel her breath on my cheek.

"Try to understand," she begged. "And please don't be jealous. There's no need for it, Jamie."

I smiled and kissed her but I couldn't forget the link between the three of them, the bond that excluded me. I could see no way out. Nothing in the world mattered to me as much as feeling her hand in mine and knowing that I had her trust.

We rode the Underground to the end of the Northern Line, High Barnet. I'd been there before and had a memory of space and green, the beginning of countryside. But nothing of that was to be seen when we surfaced. Nothing but fog clinging to pebbledash houses with names like *Bidawee* and

Mon Repos. Blackened acacias were trying to grow behind paling fences. A milkman driving his electric float like a charioteer directed us to Chorley Road. We skirted a bare patch of heath where undersized rabbits skeetered around in the summer. What we wanted was a large and rambling house with a bow front and a cheerless slate roof. In the back were a couple of acres of what had once been playground. The school buildings had long since gone and a hangar had been built on the edge of the old recreational ground. The two other pilots working for the outfit lived in town. Gordy was supposed to keep an eye on things in return for free living-quarters. The firm had captured most of the good racetrack business including runs to and from the Continent. Gordy was the owner's boy and completely trusted. Nobody talked about gold traffic in India or the prison sentence.

I could make out the shape of the hangar, the lights inside. The entrance doors were wide open.

We walked up a brick pathway between dripping rhododendrons to the front door. The curtains were drawn in all the downstairs windows. Emma hung her head, her hands pushed deep into the pockets of her old green coat, as I rang the doorbell. The pose was meant to demonstrate complete disapproval. The door opened suddenly, revealing Gordy in a dirty white towelling robe, his hairy legs and feet bare. He'd put on some weight since I'd seen him last. He's big and wide with the face of a buccaneer and his hair is chopped to clothes-brush length. He let us into a narrow, cheaply carpeted hallway smelling of fried bacon.

"Hi keed!" He punched me lightly on the biceps and winked at Emma.

He threw open the door of the sitting room with the elaborate manners of a maitre d'hôtel ushering two favoured customers to the best table in the house. The room might have been furnished at any rundown jumble sale.

There was a broken-backed old sofa, some bamboo knick-knacks, willow-pattern plates on the walls and a terracotta figure of the Lord Buddha.

Gordy switched on the two-bar heater and had Emma's hand to his lips before she could stop him. His wide toothed grin mocked her. His chin was greasy with what looked like bacon fat.

Emma ignored him pointedly, taking a seat close to the heater and sitting with her knees close together. I took the cigarette and light that he offered.

"Shit, Gordy, I thought you'd be ready."

He winked the eye further away from Emma and indicated the ceiling.

"It won't take a couple of minutes. I had things to do."

A cistern was flushed overhead. Emma curled her lip like a hostile terrier. I closed the door to the hallway.

"How long will it take to get to Cheltenham?"

He looked at the rugged waterproof

watch on his wrist. "An hour and a half or thereabouts."

I threw the sheaf of five-pound notes on the table between us.

"There's three hundred quid there. Take what you need."

He pushed it back at me. "Up yours, Nelly. You pay for whatever fuel we use. No more, no less." His look was reassurance that our comradeship was more important than Emma's tantrums. He flicked his cigarette into a fireplace that was already littered with dead butts.

"I'll be back in five minutes," he promised and went out, slamming the door loudly behind him. I could hear him calling to someone as he ran up the stairs.

"I don't trust that man," Emma announced, lifting her chin.

I sent my stub to join the others in the fireplace. "You talk a whole lot of crap at times."

A sarcastic smile came and went. "Oh really? Don't tell me you're going to tell your old chum that we're on the run from the police?"

I shook my head. "He won't ask and I won't tell him. That's the difference between my friends and yours."

An awkward silence was broken by the sound of Gordy coming down the stairs. He poked his head round the door.

"Ok, folks. Let's move it!"

He'd stuffed a pair of cords into old flying boots and was wearing a quilted nylon jacket with flashes. He led the way out through the back of the house, silencing the hard rock music from the radio on the kitchen table. A woman's tights and underclothing were hanging from a line suspended over the stove. He locked the back door carefully as we went out.

"That's a new lady in my life," he announced. "I hope I'm not going to regret this caper. She's on a turn-around to Tokyo and leaves in the morning."

Emma's voice was icy. "I'd have

thought she'd be the one to have regrets."

His smile was a perfect counter. "You know something, sweetheart? I've never been able to figure out what Jamie sees in you. I wouldn't give you house room."

He was yards ahead before she could think of a comeback. We crossed the glistening hardtop to the open hangar. It was a good hundred yards long and half as wide with powerful lights hanging from the convex roof. There were four parked helicopters, their fuselages painted blue-and-silver. A man in oil-blotched overalls was turning a metal drum on a lathe. The screech was lost in the sound from the amplified music.

He showed a thumb seeing Gordy, who had a couple of words with the two men servicing the machine nearest the exit. He filled in some papers and stuck them on a clipboard. Then he rolled a wheeled ladder across the floor to the cabin. He motioned us up, holding

214

the ladder for us. I sat between him and Emma. The two mechanics stepped back as Gordy hit the starter. The four-cylinder motor responded violently, the helicopter shuddering. Towels, paper and rags lifted on the benches and floor in the blast from the flailing blades. There were three non-retractable wheels with the centre on under the nose of the cabin. There wasn't much space, maybe five feet by four with a small baggage-hold behind the seat that was occupied by a racing saddle and bridle.

We taxied out into the fog and waited for a couple of minutes while Gordy fed the motor with fuel. The noise was almost deafening. He pitched his voice above it.

"I ought to be tarred and feathered for doing this but have no fear. Dan Dare's nerves are like steel and he sees like a hawk."

We took off at speed, climbing vertically and leaving our stomachs behind. Wipers skated over the perspex windshield and the fog lightened to pearly mist. Suddenly we were above it all, in brilliant sunshine under a cloudless sky. The limpid quality of light accentuated the starved winter look of our faces.

"Go ahead and smoke if you like," said Gordy. "Do whatever you want just so you don't fall out. It's a long long way down, a couple of thousand feet."

Emma did her number again, turning her head away deliberately, but Gordy just winked as she snuggled up close to me. Women seem to be jealous of a man's friendship with another man. It may work the other way round but if so I've never been aware of it. Gordy pulled the headphones down over his short black hair. For the next hour or so he ignored us completely. My fantasy was that the helicopter would just keep on going, bathed in sunshine, our destination somewhere a thousand miles away from Legge, Shane, Gagan and company. An island where Emma and I could forget the events of the last few days. She was suddenly very dear to me in spite of her obstinacy. All the scraps of love that I'd found before added up to nothing compared to what I had found with her.

When Gordy finally did break silence he banked the helicopter and pointed down at the brilliant cotton clouds.

"That's Cheltenham down there. Where exactly do you people need to be dropped?"

He said it deadpan, like a taxi-driver asking a fare for instructions. "I can put you down on the racetrack," he added. "I've done it a dozen times."

"That'll be great," I said.

He took off the headphones and threw them on the facia shelf. They were still broadcasting snatches of jumbled conversation. It was coming up time for the one o'clock news. At any moment the latest development in the Legge disappearance might come on the air. I had visions of Gagan heading a posse to the disused Underground

Station, of reporters and photographers crowding round the entrance as the gruesome remains were carried out on a stretcher, covered with a blanket. CANADIAN STUNTMAN AND GIRL-FRIEND SOUGHT IN SLAYING.

The light started to fade very quickly. We dropped through pearl to grey and finally into the murk that seemed to be covering the entire southern half of the country. Gordy's face was intent, his eye on the altimeter, his hands white-knuckled on the control stick. He felt his way down with the delicacy of a mosquito alighting. There was a slight jar and we had made a perfect three-point landing. Gordy switched off the motor and slid back his door. Raw air flooded into the overheated cabin. His forehead and scalp were wet with sweat. He bared his teeth, shaking his head in self-admiration.

"My *God*, what a flyer!"

It took a few seconds before my eyes started to focus then gradually the massive stands appeared through the fog. He'd put the helicopter down slap in the middle of the steeplechase track about fifty yards from the winning post.

I gave him my hand. "Thanks for everything, Gordy. I'll be in touch."

"Sure," he answered. "I'll bill you for the fuel we use." His face was as serious as it ever is. "You're not in some kind of shit, are you, Jamie?"

It would have helped to talk and I could have wished for no better listener but I lied because I had to.

"Nothing heavy, no. It's just a personal matter."

I unfastened the catch by Emma's elbow and pulled her door back. I went out first, bracing myself on the sodden turf to catch Emma as she landed. We trotted over towards the stands and ducked under the rails. The helicopter motor clattered to life again and we watched it lift into the air. The noise of its passage echoed in the empty stands and there was a rush of air on our faces. Then the aircraft seemed to dissolve and we were alone on the empty track. I raised Emma's chin, forcing her to look at me.

"Are you ok?"

The freckles stood out on her cold peaked face. "I've lost my directions. I've no idea where we are."

I tucked her arm under mine. "Near Prestbury. There's bound to be a bus-service or maybe we can call for a cab."

We walked past silent tote buildings and the bronze tribute to Arkle, in the direction of the exits. All the gates and turnstiles were locked. The only way out I could think of was across the track and into the country. We were twenty yards or so on our way when vague shapes in the fog became two uniformed policemen wearing flat caps and slickers. One had a moustache that gave him a slightly sinister air and carried a walkie-talkie. He spoke with a West Country burr, inspecting my jeans and muddied sneakers.

"Lost your way then, have you?"

The answer was compounded of fear, frustration and nerves. "I don't think that's any of your business." I'd used the expression before with Gagan and regretted it as soon as I'd opened my mouth.

But the damage was done. The men exchanged glances and drifted a fraction nearer.

"Well in the first place you're on enclosed premises," said the one with the moustache.

I gave him a placatory smile, trying desperately to regain lost ground.

"You must have heard the helicopter. We just got out of it."

"Not much of a day for flying, is it?" he asked.

I shrugged. "Fair enough, but it happened to be the only way we could get here from London."

"Got business here then, have you?" His partner's voice was rich and deep with a hint of vintage port.

It took a few seconds before the name I needed dropped into my consciousness, the name of a racehorse trainer with stables in Cheltenham.

"I've come down to see Major Farrell. As a matter of fact, I'm looking for a horse."

The glance that passed between them gave me a little hope. The one with the moustache was obviously the spokesman.

"That may well be but the point is who gave you authority to land on the racecourse? There's a right and a wrong way of doing these things. You have to have proper authority."

I hesitated but there was no other way out. In any case, Gordy would be thirty miles away by now.

"The pilot made all the flight arrangements. I know nothing at all about them."

He kept playing with the switch on his walkie-talkie as though trying to make up his mind about us. Then he nodded.

"Well I'll have to have his name and address. I'm talking about the pilot. Yours too *and* the owners of the aircraft."

I searched my pockets and gave him my driving licence. It didn't seem the moment to produce my passport. He copied the details into his notebook and took down the other particulars. I could imagine what Gordy was going to say when the local police contacted him.

The cop swung round on Emma. "How about you, Miss. Where do you live?"

"The address is the same as this gentleman's." Her voice was perfectly steady, courteous though she wasn't backing off an inch. "And my name is Emma Stafford."

This too he wrote down. When he put his notebook away, his face was pleasant enough.

"Sorry about all this but regulations is regulations and there's been a lot of Pakis coming in by air down Bristol way. How did you reckon on getting to Major Farrell's place? It's a good six miles from here."

I felt that we were almost off the hook. "We hoped that there'd be buses or possibly a cab. Our main concern is to get some lunch."

He called in on his walkie-talkie set, employing a code that was unintelligible. He snapped it off and grinned.

"We'll give you a lift into town."

My toes curled and I was apprehensive but it was impossible to refuse. Emma's face showed no more than a vague distaste and boredom. We followed the two men through a wicket-gate that I had missed near the main exit. A blue and white patrol car was drawn up on the grass outside. We climbed into the back. The man with the moustache took the wheel, his partner sitting beside him. The shelf behind the back seat was littered with maps, rolls of peppermints and a couple of flashlights. Something about our benefactors gave me the feeling that we had chanced on two of Cheltenham's finest, ready for any emergency.

I grinned up at the rearview mirror. The face there nodded. "Going to have a bit of a job getting back to London, aren't you? There's only been one train through this morning and that was four hours late."

It was something I hadn't even thought about. "We'll play it by ear. If the worst comes to the worst we can always stay overnight."

He nodded and skidded the patrol car off the grass onto the wet tarmac. The ride into town was eerie. Yellow lights mysteriously set in the fog glowed like owls' eyes. Shrouded figures moved like stage phantoms in front of the dimly lighted shop fronts. The driver finally trod on the brakes. There was little noise apart from the sound of the motor — a boy's whistle, a cracked and muffled church-bell, the lash of passing tyres.

The driver reached back and unfastened my door. "That's it then. There's a good place to eat right across the road."

It looked like it. *The Golden Hart* was a seventeenth century coaching inn with black vinegar timbers and a cobbled courtyard. The pleasant faced woman in reception smiled at us across a bowl of hyacinths.

"Good afternoon, sir. May I help you?"

"It's for lunch," I explained. "We'd like to clean up and is there a phone that I could use?"

She indicated a glass-screened room where an open fire was burning. The air was sweet with the smell of apple logs. The local gentry were out in force, dressed in twin sets and pearls and old baggy tweeds. They all appeared to be drinking large pink gins and suspended their conversation in favour of making a thorough examination of our bearing and attire. I was conscious of having tracked in mud across the floral carpet, of smelling like a wet dog and appearing where I was not wanted. On the other hand Emma traded stares with them, displaying a confidence that had them breaking for cover.

The phone booth was in the corner of the room. Emma squeezed in beside me.

"I hope you know what you're doing," she said.

I glanced down at her, holding my place in the local telephone directory. She'd used a little make-up in the car, putting it over the bruise on her cheek where Legge had hit her. Incredibly enough she was able to smile.

"I know exactly what I'm doing," I told her. "You're the one who doesn't seem to understand. That cop took our names and address. I gave him a reason for being in Cheltenham. All he has to do to find out if I'm lying is speak into the goddam box he was carrying. *That*'s why I'm calling this number."

"Too much television," she said, shaking her head at me. "A combination of that and having been an actor. You dramatize everything."

I found the entry and dialled. A woman's voice answered. It was the secretary. I gave her my name.

"I understand that Major Farrell has a hunter for sale."

There was a long pause. "A *hunter*? Are you quite sure that you have the correct number?"

"I think so, yes. Major Farrell, Boughton Stables."

"I'm afraid there is some mistake," she said. "The only hunters here belong to Major Farrell's wife and they're certainly not for sale. I'm sorry."

Emma cocked her head, mocking me as I put the phone down. I neither understood nor appreciated her attitude. We were both still jammed in the phone booth.

"Listen," I begged. "I've said this before. This isn't a game. Everything that you and I have together is at risk, Emma. Can't you understand that?"

She took off the woollen cap and shook her hair free. "That's entirely possible but not for the reasons you think."

I knew precisely what she was

saying. She was saying that Shane was blameless and that to believe otherwise was a quick way of losing her love. Every time she put me in the balance against her brother the weight came down on his side. I let my breath go and some of my heart went with it.

"Ok, let's get cleaned up."

I found the men's room and wiped most of the mud from my sneakers. Hot water and soap freshened my face, head and hands. I was beginning to wish that I'd never called Gordy Grant. The smart thing — the right thing — would have been to drag Emma bodily to Patrick Joseph O'Callaghan and make a clean breast of everything. The trouble was that I no longer seemed to have the sense to do the smart or the right thing. I was digging my own grave as fast as I could and using both feet on the job.

I dried my hands and transferred our passports and the money in my anorak pockets. I guess what I really hoped for at that moment was that we'd find Shane missing. Without him, there was a chance to explain ourselves, to show how reasonably innocent people can accidently involve themselves with disaster.

There were pamphlets about Cheltenham on a rack near the reception desk and I took one. Emma came across the lounge, elegant in spite of her shabby clothes, head up and looking straight ahead, ignoring the renewed curiosity from the occupants of the armchairs.

A Spanish waiter led us to a table. We ordered haphazardly. Food was something to be eaten rather than enjoyed. I opened the pamphlet. There was a map inside. Emma turned the paper sideways so that we could both see it and traced a route with her forefinger. Her hands are beautifully proportioned, with sensitive fingers locking into strong narrow palms.

She glanced up, hair falling over an eye. "Here's Woodmancote. You see this lane by the side of the church that's marked? Well the house is halfway down, about a quarter of a mile from the main road."

There was a key at the foot of the map. A bus-route was indicated as serving Woodmancote, the depot located about half a mile from the *Golden Hart*. We hurried through our meal, drinking only water. The armchairs in the lounge were still stuffed with replete bodies. Coffee-pots, brandy and port bottles studded the tables. Tattersall vests and corsets had been discreetly loosened. The faces of their owners were ruddied by the heat of the fire.

I called the bus depot and was told that services were running though well behind schedule. A bus for Woodmancote would be leaving in twenty minutes. The idea of using public transport, the prospect of anonymity, pleased me. We had been too long in the limelight.

"We'd better board this bus separately," I said to Emma. "And sit apart. I'll

231

watch for you getting off."

She nodded and her voice was its old sweet self. "I'm sorry if I upset you, Jamie. Help me this time and I'll never ask again, I promise you."

I looked at her and saw the woman I loved. "There'll never be another you, Emma. I want you to know that whatever happens."

The fog had lifted outside, baring the bones of the houses. The bus depot was on a sad exit to the town, twenty acres of wet asphalt decorated with strips of concrete pavement and cement shelters. Posters covered with graffiti offered trips to places like Rhyl, Exmouth and the Channel Islands. We waited in a bay near a cafeteria where disconsolate bumpkins clustered round the jukebox. A lone Pakistani in a dirty white jacket stood behind the counter, dispensing eggs-and-chips and cokes.

A single-decker bus pulled into the bay and we boarded. The passengers including old age pensioners carrying their weekend shopping, a couple of village girls touched with hysteria, the usual complement of mothers and runny-nosed children and an elderly man with a Jack Russell terrier. Emma took a seat up front close to the driver-conductor.

The fog had dispersed as if by magic, leaving the streets and buildings glistening in the pale sunshine, catching people offguard. Lights were still burning everywhere. The man holding the terrier in his lap assessed me from across the aisle, leaned towards me and spoke.

"I can see you're thinking the same thing as I am. Ah yes, the weather has changed in these islands. It's all this messing about with the planets. I wrote an article last year. They wouldn't publish it, of course."

His voice was educated, the colour and texture of his face like the shell of a walnut. His tweed jacket was patched at the elbows and bound where the sleeves had frayed. His trousers were on the short side and he was wearing a striped regimental tie.

"Is that right?" I murmured politely. I suspected an eccentric but crackpot or not, country people spoke to one another freely.

The token response was enough. He leaned forward, enclosing the terrier's jaws with his thumb and forefinger. The animal's small baleful eyes challenged me to make any untoward move.

"They've disturbed the weather-cycles," its owner confided. "I expect you know the effects of Strontium 90. The buggers won't listen."

The bus driver was heading back towards the racetrack. The stands shone in the distance. Gordy would be in London by now. I could only hope that there'd be no repercussions. The two girls sitting behind me had stopped giggling and were shamelessly eavesdropping on our conversation. I had the feeling that my neighbour was a regular passenger on the route. He nodded confidentially, his bald head trimmed with white and covered with liver-coloured blotches.

"I'm an old soldier, you know and I've seen too much of it. Two bloody wars. The next one will mean the end of civilization. Such as we know it anyhow."

He turned away abruptly and stared out of the window, the Jack Russell grumbling softly from his knees. The interlude left me unaccountably depressed. We were well past the racetrack by now and the road climbed steeply. A sign read WOODMANCOTE 2 MILES. The hills on each side were covered with what looked like beech woods. The driver pulled to the verge and stopped. The village was half a mile on. All I could see was a church and a graveyard. Emma was already out and walking. I stood in the aisle. The man with the terrier blocked my way. He nodded to the driver, donned a corduroy cap and climbed down from the bus. He touched the peak of his cap to me.

"Good day to you, sir."

He dropped the Jack Russell, its short stiff legs scrabbling long before it hit the ground. It charged off towards the churchyard. The bus went on. I bent down and retied the laces in my sneakers. The man and his dog were out of sight when I straightened up. Emma turned left into a lane without looking back. I followed. A path skirted the churchyard to a cottage set in a blighted apple-orchard. The church had lichen on the tombstones, faded paint and a general air of neglect. Emma was waiting round the first bend in the lane.

"Who was that man?" she demanded.

I fell into step with her. "Some nut. You're sure you've got the right place?"

A line of telegraph poles marked the line of the lane. There were cowpats on the ground, the fresh smell of wet grass, the rustle of scurrying blackbirds but no sign of a human being.

She nodded, pulling off her cap, freeing her hair and striding out.

"It's not very far."

It was much warmer with vapour rising from the grass verges. "Your brother certainly has an eye for choosing locations," I said unthinkingly.

But she looked at me strangely as if I were someone she'd just invented.

"What do you intend to do about Shane?"

I shook my head. "You like a rigged game, don't you?"

"No more than you do," she said. "You insisted on coming here with me. I want to know your intentions."

I stopped in my tracks. We were standing in the deep-cut lane, the hawthorn hedges higher than our heads. There was no sound of traffic at all. We were completely alone.

"I have to know what really happened," I said obstinately.

"And then what?"

We had always been honest with one another after our fashion and it worried me to think that I was becoming some kind of con artist, mouthing all kinds of insincere horseshit rather than face the truth. Whatever the truth was. I raised a hand and let it fall.

"What's the good of talking, Emma. Let's get it over."

We walked close, our rubbersoled shoes making no sound. I was losing heart with each yard we covered. She backtracked like a hound, her voice quiet but determined.

"Suppose — just *suppose* — that Shane did kill the driver. What would you do?"

My mouth was filled with frustration. "What the fuck *could* I do? Talk to him, I suppose. Try to make him see reason."

"Like spending the rest of his life in jail? This is my brother, Jamie. Is that what you mean by seeing reason?"

I grabbed her arm and swung her so that she faced me. "You know the truth as well as I do, don't you?"

"Let me go," she demanded. "You're hurting my arm."

My grasp on her loosened. There was

no need to say anything more. We both understood and each would do what he had to do. The fields about us were under corn. The beech woods beyond them shone copper in the wan sunlight. There was no grazing near but the state of the ground meant that cows were driven up and down the lane. There had to be a farm somewhere near. A noise in the hedge stopped us both in our tracks. A shower of dirt came through the bottom of the hawthorn, spattering us. I climbed onto the bank and peered through. The Jack Russell was humped in the field facing a rabbit hole, its front legs flying. Watching, I had a sensation of being watched and lifted my head slowly. My friend from the bus was craning forward so that he could see down into the lane. Our eyes met and he looked from me to Emma, his wrinkled old face curious.

"Hello again," I said, waving cheerily.

His lips pursed and for a second I thought he was going to reply. But he whistled his dog instead. I scrambled further up the bank in time to see them crossing the field in the direction of the cottage behind the church.

I jumped down, annoyed rather than alarmed. He had seen us in the bus, apparently strangers to one another and now in the lane together. This didn't matter too much. A lovers' tiff would cover the fact that we had sat apart. What irritated me was the ease with which stiff ancient joints could have brought the old man sneaking up on us undetected.

Emma wiped her brow on her sleeve, her eyes troubled. "I don't like it, Jamie. Let's go back into town and call Shane from there. It's dangerous."

"Dangerous for who?"

"For Shane, of course." She climbed onto the bank and peeped through the bushes.

"Get down from there," I argued. "That old coot's no danger. If you live in a place like this and see strangers you take an interest in who they are and where they're going. It's no more

240

than that." It seemed to me that I had the right range.

She accepted my steadying hand and jumped down lightly to stand with her head on one side, hearing things I couldn't hear.

"For crissakes let's go," I said impatiently.

She turned her mouth down but obeyed. The lane turned again and the hedgerows were a dozen feet lower. A broken iron gate gave access to a twenty acre field where the corn shoots already showed green.

Emma pointed across the field. "There it is! Beyond those trees and the wall. You can just see the house!"

It was some five hundred yards away, grey-violet against the dark fringe of trees. The next bend in the lane brought us to wrought-iron gates protected by two carved lions. The gates were closed. We went through a wicket. The gravelled drive swept between ragged lawns covered with mole-hills and past an empty pool to the front of the Cotswold-stone house. The trees we had seen were oaks, winter stripped, but gnarled and burly. A flagstone wall about fifteen feet high encircled the oaks and the unkempt garden. We walked up the driveway. Its curve took us out of sight of the entrance from the lane.

The house was built in traditional Cotswold style with end chimneys and a gable on each side of the nail-studded front door. I kept my eyes on the latticed and curtained windows as we neared the house. I could see no sign of Shane. If he was in there he was keeping well out of the way. Rain and wind had plastered last year's leaves against the bottom of the front door and the broad steps leading up to it. The windows were rain-streaked and filthy, the garden uncared for. The hope rose that maybe Shane wasn't here after all. That he had been and gone, telling Emma to get here as fast as she could as a ploy for him to gain time. I scraped some of the caked leaves away with my toe, revealing the crust of dirt sealing the door.

"Nobody's used this for months."

She made no answer, standing with her back against the wall as I stepped onto the flowerbed and looked through the nearest window. Flimsy curtains behind the velvet drapes made it impossible to see into the room. I rang the doorbell but there was no answer.

A rook croaked a warning in the oaks and twenty other birds flew up. The flock wheeled and made off into the setting sun. Although we were miles from anywhere once again I had the feeling that we were being watched. I glanced back across the fields instinctively, half expecting to see the old man and his dog but there was nothing there but the earth and the corn.

"Let's try the back," I suggested.

She locked her fingers tightly in mine. We walked through a stable yard where the looseboxes were filled with logs and outdoor furniture, past a kitchen garden with netting sagging on broken canes. The back door was flanked by an overflowing rain barrel and an empty kennel. I peeped through red-checked curtains into a large kitchen with plenty of room for the deep freezer unit and the washing machine. The sink looked clean but I noticed that the electric clock near the dresser was still working. It was nearly three o'clock.

I turned the handle of the back door. It was unlocked. A closer inspection of the kitchen showed that someone had been there recently. There was a loaf in the breadbin, some butter, cheese and milk in the icebox. Emma hadn't moved from her place near the table, following every movement that I made. A second door opened into a panelled corridor hung with framed prints of birds of prey. The corridor ran the length of the house and was lighted by end windows. It was cold though sunshine streamed across the grey Wilton carpet.

I shouted Shane's name. My voice tumbled back from the hallway. I moved forward cautiously, like a man testing ice, Emma hanging onto the back of my anorak. God knows what we expected to find. The curtains were drawn on the windows each side of the front door. There was just enough light to make out the marble busts on the floor, Boehm fledglings on the mantel over the fireplace. There was a phone on a side table but nothing to indicate that the house was being lived in, none of the usual stuff you'd expect to find. No coats, no hats, no mail or newspapers.

A dark polished banister twisted up to the second floor, the stair carpet a warm red against cream paint. I opened the panelled door in front of me. A pair of Purdey guns was racked on the wall. There were wading boots and fishing-tackle, a fox-mask grinning in a glass case. We both whirled as somebody spoke behind us.

Shane was leaning in the doorway across the hall, smiling. He must have been in the front room since we arrived. I could see no other way in which he could have got there.

Emma broke away from me quickly, throwing her arms around her brother's neck and bringing his face down to hers. He looked at me over her shoulder, a day's growth on his face and his red hair wild.

"Hello, Jamie!"

He was wearing the clothes I'd last seen him in, dark pants, a polo-necked sweater and leather jacket. We followed him into what looked like a drawing room. It was a mixture of old and new. Japanese silk walls, a faded and much-mended Aubusson on the floor, silver trinkets displayed on a marble-topped stand. There were books about painting and flower-arrangements, some Beardsley erotica and a few novels. A heater was blowing hot air from the empty fireplace. It was obvious that Shane had been sleeping in the room. There were blankets on the high-winged chintz sofa. He pulled Emma down on them, keeping an arm around her shoulders protectively. He grinned affably, like a host concerned for belated guests.

"How did you manage to get here?"

"By helicopter," I said. "Someone I know."

He nodded. His eyes were brighter than ever I'd seen them. The picture of Sara that had been missing from his bedroom was on a table near the sofa. The flimsy curtains inside the drapes were open in the end window. I could see the rooks back in the trees, a sentinel posted on the highest branch.

"We landed on the racetrack. A couple of cops in a patrol car gave us a lift into Cheltenham." I explained what had happened. I didn't want to hide anything from him. All I needed was to establish the truth between us. "Then we took the bus out."

The hand he was holding Emma with was never still, his fingers constantly kneading her shoulder. She looked at me almost defiantly.

"You should never have come here, Jamie," he said suddenly.

"You mean me or both of us?" I countered.

"I mean you."

It intrigued me how he had got here. It might have been possible to drive in spite of the fact that half the country had been fogged-under for the last twenty-four hours. The same fog that had helped him creep up on a man coming home and then kill him. There was no sign of his car outside but there were plenty of buildings where he might have hidden it.

He shook his head slowly. "You shouldn't have come here," he repeated.

I dragged smoke into my lungs and held it there before exhaling. "You said that before. Things have changed, Shane. Where Emma goes, I go."

The scar on his forehead was livid. "That sounds like a hostile statement, Jamie. Was it meant to be?"

The resemblance between them was uncanny. It wasn't so much the red hair and green eyes, the freckled skin, as an impression of unity that they projected. I'd never noticed it quite so much when Sara had been alive.

Emma was looking straight at me but her words were for her brother.

"Jamie thinks that you killed the driver." She said it almost indulgently, in the tone of a mother who catches her child with his hand in the cookie-jar.

He removed his arm and went to the window, gazing out across the ragged lawns and empty drive. When he finally did turn, the intervening seconds had changed his expression completely. He looked like a man who had wrestled hard and long with a problem but then had solved it. He crossed the room and opened a cabinet.

"There's scotch," he said over his shoulder. "And some ginger wine and that's it."

"I don't want either," I said.

He smiled as if my answer held no

real significance. "Get some glasses and water from the kitchen, Emma," he ordered quietly. She left the room immediately.

He wandered a few steps in my direction. "Do the police know that I'm here?"

I shook my head. "Not from me. But they're certainly looking for you. In fact they want to see us both. Gagan called this morning."

"And you told him nothing?" His tone was sharp.

"That's right," I replied. "I told him nothing."

He gave me a sly look. "Why did you come down here, Jamie? What exactly is it that you want from me?"

"The truth," I said. "Let's stop with the bullshit. I want a straight answer. Did you or didn't you kill the driver?"

His back seemed relieved of some invisible weight.

"You know something, there are people whose death doesn't matter at all. And then there are people whose death leaves the world a poorer place, people like Sara. My world went with her, Jamie. Are you able to take that in or not?"

I shrugged. "I think so, yes. Certainly I knew how you felt about her. I know how Emma felt too. But Sara's gone and nothing can bring her back."

"You don't understand, do you?" he said.

"I was an outsider," I told him. "But not any longer. And I have the right to know my involvement. We're down to the business of survival, Shane."

Emma was back, carrying a tray, glasses and a pitcher of water. Shane poured scotch for all of us. I took the glass he offered and he sat down on the sofa again, holding Emma's hand.

"I want you both to listen to me," he said. "And try to understand."

Adrenalin poured into my bloodstream. I knew instinctively that this was to be his confession. More than that I knew what was wrong with him.

I guess I must have known or at least guessed it for some time. I remembered the night that Sara's body had been found, the look on his face, stunned and disbelieving. I remembered how Emma had lain beside me, secretly weeping. I'd wondered then whether the flaw in Sara's make-up was mirrored in her twin. Who's to say whether both of them were crazy but one thing I *was* sure of, their minds had crossed a line that was forbidden territory to the rest of us.

Emma's fingers were held against his cheek now. "I'm wrong," he said, looking at me. "I can't expect you to understand, Jamie. Only Emma understands. She knows that part of me died with Sara."

There were tears in his eyes as he spoke. Tears for himself, I suspected. I found myself feeling absolutely nothing for him, neither pity nor disgust. I'm wrong. I was scared of him. It was Emma I was concerned with. She must have accepted his guilt from the start. The rest had been a show put on for me and stemmed from her fierce protectiveness towards him. Sara might have gone but she was still there to take care of him.

"I killed that man for all of us," he said calmly. "I *had* to kill him. He was the only witness against us."

A kind of relief flooded me. It was out in the open at last.

"They were going to show him pictures in the morning." He was talking with movements of his hands, like a schoolteacher in front of his class. "Our pictures could have been among them. I couldn't have risked offering him money. There was no other way. I just *had* to do it, Jamie."

My impression was that he was talking to Emma rather than to me. That he didn't, in fact, give a goddam what I thought, one way or another. There was a ghoulish kind of logic in what he said but it wasn't exactly reassuring. We were all getting tarred with the same filthy brush.

"You murder a man in cold blood," I challenged. "And claim that you did it for *us*? Not for me, you didn't!"

We continued to stare at one another for what seemed eternity. Brother, sister and outsider. The rooks outside were airborne again, wheeling and planing noisily. There was this strange overriding feeling that something momentous was about to happen. It had been there with me ever since I entered this house.

Emma pulled her brother close. "We're going to help you, darling. Whatever you decide to do, we'll help you."

Her eyes flicked sideways at me. And if he decided to kill someone else, I thought. Would we help in that too? Her face was against his. It was impossible for her to see the cunning in his look.

"I've got an idea that Gagan is on to us," he said. "He suspects but he can't put the pieces together."

"He suspects all right," I answered.

"I already told you. He called this morning. He wants us both round at the police station."

The vague smile slid from his face. "Did he mention me specifically?"

"You're damn right he did. We were both round at your place when he called. Emma spoke to him."

"Is that true?" he demanded.

She moved her head up and down. "He left a message. He wanted you to get in touch with him right away."

He came to his feet frowning, drawn again by the windows. Then he swung round behind an outstretched forefinger.

"As long as we stick together there's nothing they *can* do! By the time they find Legge — *if* they find him — we'll all be as dead as he is anyway. And there's nothing in this world that can connect me with the taxi-driver. The invisible man. Nobody saw me. Nobody heard me."

Nobody but the man he had killed. So there it was, the whole nightmarish scheme, the way he planned it. We were going to spend the rest of our lives sitting on secret knowledge of murder. With no penance, no regret and, I guess in time, not even a memory.

I looked up, wanting no mistake to be made. "I'm not going along with you, Shane. I can't."

He didn't seem to have heard but walked across to the cabinet, clicking his thumb and forefinger. He poured himself another scotch and retraced his steps.

"The bus," he said over the top of his glass. "Did anyone else get off with you?"

Emma moved on the nest of blankets. "Some old man with a Jack Russell terrier. I think he lives in that cottage behind the church. He cut across the fields after us and watched us down the lane."

Shane put his glass down very carefully. "Shit! That's Colonel Mead. He's a real old busybody. Crazy enough but his head works well enough when he wants it to. The thing is that he'd know that this house is supposed to be empty and there's no other place for you to have come but the farm."

It seemed that they wanted to talk about anything but murder. "What are you going to do, Shane?" I asked quietly.

He looked at me, puzzled. "Do about what?"

I shook my head. "You've killed a man, for crissakes. You can't expect to get away with it."

"Why not?" he asked bluntly. "What the fuck do you think I killed him for, to give myself up? Is *that* what you think? No, Jamie. We're all going to spend a nice quiet weekend together, working things out, then on Monday we go back to London. If Gagan wants to see me, he knows where to find me."

I held out my hand to Emma. "You realize that he's crazy, don't you? You're right when you say the guy needs help. He's sick, baby. As sick as his sister was."

Emma reared up like a swamp snake preparing to strike but Shane was in first, his face white and dangerous.

"What do you know about families, you jealous bastard? What do you know about any of us? Nothing!"

I pulled the bundle of banknotes from my pocket and threw it on the table. It would be a cheap way out if it worked.

"I don't know if you need this or not but take it anyway. From now on you're on your own, Shane. I've lowered the curtains on this one as far as Emma and I are concerned. I'm taking her back to London now. Tomorrow morning we'll go to the police with Patrick Joseph O'Callaghan. On your feet Emma!"

The moment was here at last. Each of us knew it. Time stretched in our brains till Emma's fingers moved, lingering on Shane's drawn face.

"Don't worry, my darling. It'll be all

right. It won't be as bad as you think. Patrick Joseph will help."

"Are you coming, Emma?" I counted ten in my head. Then another ten.

She stayed where she was, her lips saying something inaudible. I guessed at 'please' but couldn't be sure. I was genuinely sorry for Shane in that second. I'd forgotten that the seed of defeat is sown in every victory.

"So long, Shane," I said and waited for Emma to get up.

It was Shane who rose, coming up fast, holding the gun he had concealed under a cushion.

"You're not going anywhere, you fucker. You're staying right here till I decide the best thing to do with you."

My thinking processes had stopped completely for the moment, stunned by the turnaround that left Emma with Shane instead of me. She made no effort to avoid my eyes as Shane gun-shoved me into the hallway. Her face was as blank as a post office clerk's. I backed off under Shane's prodding as far as the stairwell. A closet was built under the stairs. He wrenched it open and sent me staggering into the darkness. I just had time to see the stout old-fashioned lock then the door was slammed on me. By extending my arms I could touch the walls and felt brooms and a carpet-sweeper. There was a strong smell of floor polish. I put my ear against the crack in the door. The house was full of whispers. I slumped down on the floor, using something soft from a hook as a cushion.

My fight with Emma was lost. All I could hope for now was to save my life. I was morally certain that Shane intended to kill me. To a man as crazy as he was another killing would mean nothing. He had already crossed the psychological barrier and wouldn't even have to justify my death. I could imagine how it would be done. He would drive me up into the woods and leave me there with a bullet in my brain. And Emma would weep. Or maybe not. I could no longer be sure of anything.

I sat on the floor in the darkness, nursing a dull resentment and a determination to do Shane as much damage as I could before he put me away for good. My attack would have to be made through subterfuge. I was physically bigger and stronger than he was but he was the one on the right end of the gun. My thoughts kept describing circles with Emma always at their centre. There had been no pressure on her from Shane at the last. She had been free to make whatever decision she chose. I'd told her to come and she'd stayed, proving finally that her love and loyalty for her brother was stronger than whatever it was that she felt for me.

I leaned sideways, still on the floor, putting my ear to the crack in the door again. The drawing room door had been left open. I could hear the two of them talking, Shane's voice sliding up and down as it did when excited.

My cigarettes and lighter were in my pocket. The tiny flame illuminated the interior of the broom closet. The walls were the reverse sides of the pine panelling. There was no plaster on the ceiling, just the wooden framework of the staircase and the underparts of the treads. It would have been physically possible to batter a way out through there even without tools. But the first sound Shane heard would bring him in to attend to me that much quicker.

Time passed. I grew tired of looking at my watch and sticking my ear against the door. I was conscious that the hallway was growing darker. It's true that the loss or suspension of one of the senses heightens the powers of the others. I couldn't see but my nose and ears were that much sharper. The smell of cheese toasting and tea brewing was unmistakable. It seemed a long time since I had eaten but nothing was served to me. The conversation in the drawing room came in bursts. They seemed to be arguing. A couple of times, Shane actually shouted. It was warm in the closet and I must have dozed off. When I checked my watch again it was after nine o'clock.

I clambered up, hearing footsteps crossing the hallway. The key turned in the lock and the door was thrown open. The only light in the hallway came from the drawing room. Emma was standing directly in front of her brother, her body between Shane and me. I looked into the eyes of a complete stranger.

"You're being given a chance," she said. "I've given my word that you'll take it."

I wet my lips cautiously. "A chance to do what?"

"To save your life," she said steadily.

"I like it," I said. "Especially coming from you." The bitterness driving the words had registered. I could see it in her eyes.

Shane's face showed above her shoulder, hard and implacable. I couldn't see the gun in his hand but I knew it was there.

"Shane wants you to help him move Legge's body," said Emma. She was no more than a couple of feet away from me, standing just outside the entrance to the broom closet.

It came to me that Shane must be really worried about Gagan. If the police suspected Shane sufficiently to search Lennox Gardens they would certainly find that the Highgate store was on his books. From that to searching the Underground station was simple progression.

"You've got to be strong," she declaimed. And there was something strange in her voice. "If we're all strong and we stick together no harm can come to us. Don't you see that, Jamie?"

She pushed her hands out towards me as though she was pleading and what I did see were the couple of inches of steel protruding from her coat sleeve. It was the chased blade of an ornamental dagger that had been in the drawing room. Only then it had been in a sheath. She must have found time and the opportunity to remove it.

I suddenly realized that the scene before me had been a charade. That she was doing her best to save my life. Shane moved before I had time to take the blade, almost as though he had read the truth in my face. He spun Emma violently and kicked the dagger across the hallway as it fell to the floor. A shell smashed into the wall inches away from my head. My ears sang and the closet was filled with explosion.

Shane's face was frenzied. "You whore!" he screamed. "Bitch!"

He rocked her with blows to the face, using the flat of his hand and holding the gun on me with the other. He sent her sprawling into the closet beside me and locked the door. I could hear his breathing outside, as loud as the banging of my heart. Then I heard him cross the hallway to the drawing room. My arms found Emma's shaking body. Her tears were wet on my face. I did my best to comfort her, guessing what must have been going through her mind. She knew Shane better than anyone else alive. She must have sensed that he was becoming psychopathic and protected him out of her love and loyalty. To be ripped in half the way she had been and then lose everything was too much for someone like Emma. Courage she certainly had. She also had love.

She wiped her eyes in the darkness, sniffing. "He'll kill us both, I'm sure of it. Especially now that he thinks that I've betrayed him."

I held her even tighter, wanting to protect her. "I'll think of something," I whispered, the promise as much to myself as to her.

Her head lifted. "I wanted to come when you told me to but I guessed what he'd do. I thought I could talk him round. The dagger was stupid. I just wasn't thinking properly, desperate."

"That guy outside isn't Shane," I said. "You've got to keep telling yourself that. It's someone else. Someone we don't know."

Sadness filled her voice, stripping her of all pretence. "What difference does it make? All I want is to live and be happy with you."

"We'll make it somehow," I said. Seconds later I yelled on impulse. "*Shane!*"

The echo died, leaving the tick of the tall clock in the hallway suddenly very loud. I put my mouth to the crack in the door and shouted again.

"Emma's hurt, Shane. Open up!"

I heard him cross the hallway then the door was unlocked. The flesh on his face seemed to have shrunk, making his eyes even wilder. He had taken one of the twelve-bores from the gunroom and both barrels were trained on my belly. Emma was crouching at my feet, her face hidden in her hands. There was no possibility of jumping him. At that range he'd have cut us in half.

"She's your sister, Shane," I urged.

He moved his head from side to side. "She's your whore not my sister. She never has been, you bastard, since you appeared on the scene!"

I tried one last time. "Do whatever you have to with me but let her go."

"Bollix!" He rolled one lip over another. "No, you had your chance, both of you. Now you can make the most of what's left."

He closed the door with the shotgun barrels and turned the key. Emma came up beside me. Cold sweat was dripping from my armpits and my hands were unsteady. I strained my ears, hearing the faintest of creaks outside. Shane was creeping catfooted down the corridor towards the kitchen. Seconds later, I heard the back door open and shut.

"That's it! He's getting the car!" I pulled her with me so that our backs were against the wall. "When I say so, kick as hard as you can."

We linked arms and braced our bodies. "*Now!*" We both jumped, our feet landing simultaneously. The door shuddered but held. "Again!" I urged. She gasped as she launched her legs.

This time the door flew open with a sound like a pistol shot, leaving the lock hanging from splintered wood. I grabbed her hand and dragged her along the corridor opposite and burst through the nearest door. The furniture was swathed in dustsheets. From the window I could see the lights of a car in the stable yard. He must have had it concealed in one of the outbuildings. The catch released, I threw up the window. Our feet touched the flowerbeds at the same moment as the car started rolling towards the front of the house.

We were off and running, arms flailing and legs pumping, across the stable yard and old artichoke beds, heading for the clump of oak trees. There was cover there but the wall in front of us was too high to climb without some kind of ladder. I put my finger against my mouth, signalling her to stay where she was. I just managed to dash the twenty yards back to the stableyard and the car lights were extinguished. I heard Shane's walk on the gravelled driveway.

A builder's plank was lying across the manger in one of the looseboxes. I trotted back to the trees, the plank on my shoulder. Emma held it up against the wall. I crawled up, using my hands and elbows till my fingers grasped the top. One last heave and I was up, a leg on each side. I reached down, clinging to the top of the wall with my free hand. Emma grabbed my wrist and between us we made it. We landed heavily and struggled up. The hedges bordering the lane were lost in obscurity. The only guides to the highway were the telephone poles, just visible against the sky. We were halfway across the field when headlamps lighted the lane. A car was being driven very slowly in our direction.

It cruised past and stopped near the church, at the junction of the lane and the highway. Then the lights went out. I was aware of so many things. Of being scared and knowing I mustn't show it. Emma's life was in my hands and I wondered if I had what it took. The darkness that now hid us could equally help the man who was hunting us. The friendly village pub with its quiet country voices and promise of help seemed a hundred miles away.

I took Emma's arm. "We'll make for the cottage behind the church. The one where that old guy with the dog lives. When we come to the lane, put your head down and run."

She stumbled along at my side, her feet sinking in the soft moist dirt, obedient and silent. I could sense her despair. No matter what happened now she had lost her brother forever.

"It's the only way," I urged. "We've got to contact the police."

Her fingers tightened on my arm but she didn't speak. We crossed the field and the lane lay beneath us. Anything further than twenty yards away merged with the night completely, the hedges, banks and grass verges. It was now or never. The hawthorns were too dense and were spiked with thorns. It was impossible to force our way through. I spread my anorak on top and helped Emma over. I followed. We dashed through cowdung to the bank on the other side. The hedge there was tall and leaned outwards. By the time we had climbed it, our hands were scratched and bleeding.

The hillside with the beech forest lay behind us, safe possibly but unknown territory. I needed a phone. We trotted towards the highway, moving parallel to the lane. My guess was that Shane was still waiting somewhere near the T-junction. He'd have pulled his car off the road, gambling that we would head for the main road and the village.

The church loomed suddenly in the headlamps of a passing car. The lights held for a few seconds, fixing our route to the cottage. A paling fence backed with chicken wire surrounded the apple orchard. A flagged pathway led to the front door. Lamplight yellowed the windows. The dog barked as my hand touched the gate-latch. The noise was frantic as we ran over the paving stones.

I beat on the door with both fists, shouting. "Help! Open up!"

The terrier was clawing at the bottom of the door. Bolts were withdrawn, the lock unfastened. The door opened a few inches, held on a stout chain. The Colonel peered out, holding the struggling terrier firmly in his arms. He was wearing bedroom slippers and an old camelhair robe over blue flannel pyjamas.

"What do you want?" he demanded brusquely, his teeth jumping in his mouth.

The words came in a rush. "There's a man with a shotgun after us." I threw an arm in the direction of the church.

He brought his face a little nearer. "You're that fellow on the bus." It was almost an accusation.

"It's a matter of life and death," I gasped. "At least let us in!"

"I don't like your looks," he said

promptly. "Who's that you've got with you?"

I pushed Emma into the light. She was holding her mane of red hair back so that he could see her face.

"It's true, Colonel Mead," she pleaded. "My brother is trying to kill us both."

I thought he was going to slam the door in our faces but something he'd seen or sensed in Emma made him change his mind. He lifted the chain off the hook. The moment the door closed behind us, the small dog sniffed the bottoms of my jeans, dropped an ear and wagged the stump of its tail.

The room was perfect for its owner. There was a beamed ceiling, a gate-legged table and Windsor chairs, a dog-basket by the open coal fire. Pictures of Sandhurst, Tobruk and Italy were scattered around, each featuring the same lean-faced man growing older.

The Colonel pushed a chair at Emma. "How did you come to know my name, young lady?"

"My brother," she said. "He's been staying in Mrs. Sergeant's house."

There was a silver chocolate-pot on a hob in the fireplace, a mug on the small refectory table. The Jack Russell curled up in its basket, one beady eye left open and on us. A nineteen-thirties radio was playing Haydn. Colonel Mead silenced it and pointed at the chocolate-pot.

"I don't suppose this stuff will be any good to you. But it's all there is, I'm afraid. I can only afford to drink a week in the month on my pension."

I was still standing. A partly opened door led to the darkened kitchen. The room was snug, the curtains lined. There was a general air of *gemütlichkeit* but what Emma and I needed was action.

"Listen," I said. "You don't appear to grasp the situation. There's a guy out there somewhere armed with a pistol and shotgun. He knows we're somewhere in the area. I want to call the police."

He tightened the cord on his robe. The lapels were stained with egg and gravy.

"Are you two married? Engaged?"

Emma met his inspection squarely. "We live together."

I made a move towards the phone. "Drop it!" he barked. "That's an order!"

His eyebrows bristled with stiff white hairs. He must have been seventy-five but the spirit of command was in his blood. He turned to Emma, his voice much gentler.

"Suppose you tell me what this is all about, young lady."

She was sitting with her head hanging down and moved her shoulders hopelessly.

"God*dammit*, you old fool!" I burst out. "Can't you get it into your head that our lives are in danger? There's a lunatic at large and you stand there asking bullshit questions!"

He narrowed his gaze to a glare. "You speak when you're spoken to.

And if and when that happens, see you keep a civil tongue in your head! There's a lady present."

Emma looked up, shaking the hair from her face. "There's a man called Legge who is missing. You must have heard, he's a gossip-columnist."

"A useless sort of occupation. Yes, I heard."

"An evil bastard," I said. Respect had been shown to age and sooner or later I was going to use that phone. "He was engaged to Emma's sister. When she broke it off he used his column to destroy her. And I mean that literally. She killed herself."

He refilled his mug from the chocolate-pot, not missing a word, intent on what I was saying.

"We abducted him. Emma, her brother and me. Ok, it was a crazy thing to do but we wanted to teach him a lesson. We put him in an old Underground station. Now he's dead."

The Colonel's eye was bright and sharp. "Is he, by George! You mean you killed the fellow?"

"It was an accident. But the next death wasn't. I'm talking about the taxi-driver who was found asphyxiated. Emma's brother killed him."

He looked at the phone, a little apprehensively. "He's mad," said Emma.

"It won't stop there," I added. "Emma and I are the last two witnesses."

He lifted the receiver. "I want the police, the County Constabulary. Sergeant *who*? Look here, it's Colonel Mead this end. Church Cottage, Woodmancote. I want the chap in charge of your detectives."

The dog raised its head above the rim of the basket, both ears pricked and growling softly. I looked at the windows instinctively. Mead's manner was becoming impatient.

"Detective Superintendent Rimmell? Good evening, Superintendent. I've got a couple of people here at the cottage I think you should take a look at. That's right, a man and a woman.

A case of murder as I understand it. Something to do with this Legge fellow. L E G G E!" he bawled.

He covered his free ear with his hand. Whatever he heard had obviously sharpened his interest.

"No, just the two of them but there's a second man in the area, the girl's brother. Apparently he's been staying at Mrs. Sergeant's house. That's right, just down the lane from me. He's somewhere between there and the main road and he's armed. These people say that he's got an automatic pistol and a twelve-bore shotgun."

He put the phone down carefully. "They're on their way."

The terrier was up in its basket, its whole body quivering. The Colonel opened a drawer in the Welsh dresser and produced a revolver the size of a small cannon. It was a Webley 45, service issue. He broke the weapon, sighted through the barrel then spun the cylinder. I could see the copper-capped bullets.

"Put one through the bugger's backside at fifty paces if he asks for it," he said with satisfaction. His concern about the use of coarse language appeared to have been temporarily suspended.

He put the gun down on the table and swung towards the back door as the terrier launched itself into the darkened kitchen. Enough light came from the sitting room to see the shape of a figure standing outside the kitchen window. Shotgun barrels crashed through the glass. A hand reached through, groping for the key in the door. The dog's leap carried its snapping jaws close to Shane's sleeve.

The Colonel's face was stiff with anger. Half-a-dozen canes stood in an upturned drainpipe near the back door. He grabbed an ashplant and moving surprisingly quickly brought it down with all his force on the encroaching arm. A yelp of pain came from outside but Shane kept his arm where it was. His fingers turned the key before Mead could lift his stick again. Shane burst in behind the opening door, holding the shotgun waist-high.

The old man showed no fear even then, raising his cane to strike. The blast from the shotgun ripped through his chest at close quarters. He fell to his knees, stray pellets drawing blood from his leathery neck and then keeled over sideways, his heart literally blown away.

Shane's foot lifted the terrier into the night. He stepped over Mead's fallen body, his right arm dangling uselessly. His eyes were wild, his clothes and shoes soiled with dirt and mould as though he'd crawled through a badger's sett. In spite of the pain he must have been in, he was smiling as he came through the kitchen towards us.

"You first," he promised, looking at me.

They say that in moments like these your whole life flashes through your mind. All I could think of was that he'd fired one barrel, he couldn't get us both with the other.

"Run!" I yelled and kicked the gate-legged table at him.

Emma stayed where she was. The next movements were like some dream sequence. She grabbed the Colonel's revolver with both hands, aiming it shakily at her brother. The noise of the explosion was a flatter sound than the roar of the shotgun. Shane stared at her in surprise, his glazing eyes seeking hers as his mouth and throat gushed blood. The bullet had crashed through his neck, severing the main artery. The shotgun dropped and he followed heavily, his head thudding against the floor.

That was when Emma started to scream and I thought it would last for ever. She backed off towards the wall, her hands outstretched as though pushing away all she saw. Then the noise stopped. Her mouth stayed open and she was shaking violently. The terrier limped in on three legs and stretched out by its dead master.

Emma was on the edge of hysteria but I couldn't bring myself to slap her bruised and swollen face.

"It's all right," I whispered. Two people lay dead on the floor and our lives were shattered but I said it again. "It's all right, darling."

We sat with her head in my lap. She closed her eyes as I stroked her forehead gently. Hiccoughs racked her but the terrifying soundless weeping had stopped. Blood was spreading from the two bodies, Mead's soaking into the carpet. Shane's a glistening obscenity on the kitchen floor.

An atavistic urge prompted me to cover the bodies, to conceal death, but the motors had seized in my arms and legs. The terrier's head rose. Cars were coming fast along the highway. They stopped. Doors were slammed and a whistle blew. Then all was silent again. The stillness held for two or three minutes. So quiet was it that I could hear my own heart beating.

Suddenly a powerful light illuminated

the kitchen from the outside. More lights showed through the hallway windows. A ring of them was converging on the cottage. Emma lifted herself. A man shouted through a loudhailer.

"Colonel Mead!"

They must have found Shane's car and were taking no chances. I shouted back but they couldn't have heard me.

"If you're all right, show yourself, Colonel!"

The men outside were waiting for some sign of life. But all we could do was sit there and wait for them. The terrier was prone by Mead's side, its leg and spirit both broken. The back door was half open, the shattered windowpane exposed to the brilliance of the powerful lights.

A quick sudden rush of footsteps carried men through the apple orchard. They stopped near the kitchen. A heavy foot kicked the door completely open and a man charged into the cottage. He jumped the sprawling legs of Shane's body and crouched, aiming a gun at the sitting room. He was short and dark like a Welsh miner and wearing bullet-proof clothing. Another armed man covered him from the kitchen doorway. A third man came into view, his accoutrements flashing in the light. The insignia of rank showed on his cap and shoulders. He moved forward economically, carrying some kind of baton. The armed men stayed where they were, their weapons shielding him as he stared down at Shane's body.

He came into the sitting room, his eyes expressionless as he glanced down at the Colonel. The dog rose and whimpered. The Superintendent wrinkled his nose at the smell of blood.

"Who's responsible for this?" he asked quietly. There was no bluster, no threat, just a level demand for information.

Emma answered from some secret refuge, finding strength and courage.

"That's my brother outside. He killed Colonel Mead."

He whacked the baton softly against his palm. "And who killed your brother?"

"I did," she said steadily. "He was going to shoot Jamie."

The cottage was suddenly crowded with men, a dozen at least, some of them in uniform. I could hear others outside in the orchard, somebody shouting.

The Superintendent pointed at the dog. "Somebody get that animal to a vet. And get hold of Doctor Burgess and the Mobile Crime Lab. *Move!*"

The sitting room emptied. Emma and I were still sitting on the sofa, our hands touching. The Superintendent looked down at us, a countryman first then a policeman.

"They found Legge's body this afternoon."

I nodded acceptance. I'd always known that they would. "It was an accident. We only meant to teach him a lesson. Nobody wanted to kill him."

His eyes were almost kindly. "What

makes a couple of decent youngsters like you get mixed up in such a terrible business?"

I searched for an answer. Family loyalty, the love of a woman. Neither explanation was complete.

I wanted to tell him and couldn't. "I don't know."

Emma's tongue flicked over her dry lips. "I just don't understand," he said. "Four people dead and for what?"

"Will we be able to call our solicitor?" It was somehow very important that Patrick should be there, society's seal of approval on our confession.

He didn't seem to have heard but was looking down at Mead. "There's no one to miss him as far as I know. It's just as well." He turned his head again. "You'd better get your things together."

"We've got what we came with," I answered.

He nodded indifferently, his mind on other matters. "Then you're ready."

"Ready," I said. I lifted Emma to

her feet and kissed her. What I read in her eyes I knew they could never take from me.

THE END

A GENTEEL LITTLE MURDER
Philip Daniels

Gilbert had a long-cherished plan to murder his wife. When the polished Edward entered the scene Gilbert's attitude was suddenly changed.

DEATH AT THE WEDDING
Madelaine Duke

Dr. Norah North's search for a killer takes her from a wedding to a private hospital.

MURDER FIRST CLASS
Ron Ellis

Will Detective Chief Inspector Glass find the Post Office robbers before the Executioner gets to them?

A FOOT IN THE GRAVE
Bruce Marshall

About to be imprisoned and tortured in Buenos Aires, John Smith escapes, only to become involved in an aeroplane hijacking.

DEAD TROUBLE
Martin Carroll

Trespassing brought Jennifer Denning more than she bargained for. She was totally unprepared for the violence which was to lie in her path.

HOURS TO KILL
Ursula Curtiss

Margaret went to New Mexico to look after her sick sister's rented house and felt a sharp edge of fear when the absent landlady arrived.

THE DEATH OF ABBE DIDIER
Richard Grayson

Inspector Gautier of the Sûreté investigates three crimes which are strangely connected.

NIGHTMARE TIME
Hugh Pentecost

Have the missing major and his wife met with foul play somewhere in the Beaumont Hotel, or is their disappearance a carefully planned step in an act of treason?

BLOOD WILL OUT
Margaret Carr

Why was the manor house so oddly familiar to Elinor Howard? Who would have guessed that a Sunday School outing could lead to murder?

THE DRACULA MURDERS
Philip Daniels

The Horror Ball was interrupted by a spectral figure who warned the merrymakers they were tampering with the unknown.

THE LADIES
OF LAMBTON GREEN
Liza Shepherd

Why did murdered Robin Colquhoun's picture pose such a threat to the ladies of Lambton Green?

CARNABY
AND THE GAOLBREAKERS
Peter N. Walker

Detective Sergeant James Aloysius Carnaby-King is sent to prison as bait. When he joins in an escape he is thrown headfirst into a vicious murder hunt.

MUD IN HIS EYE
Gerald Hammond

The harbourmaster's body is found mangled beneath Major Smyle's yacht. What is the sinister significance of the illicit oysters?

THE SCAVENGERS
Bill Knox

Among the masses of struggling fish in the *Tecta*'s nets was a larger, darker, ominously motionless form . . . the body of a skin diver.

DEATH IN ARCADY
Stella Phillips

Detective Inspector Matthew Furnival works unofficially with the local police when a brutal murder takes place in a caravan camp.

STORM CENTRE
Douglas Clark

Detective Chief Superintendent Masters, temporarily lecturing in a police staff college, finds there's more to the job than a few weeks relaxation in a rural setting.

THE MANUSCRIPT MURDERS
Roy Harley Lewis

Antiquarian bookseller Matthew Coll, acquires a rare 16th century manuscript. But when the Dutch professor who had discovered the journal is murdered, Coll begins to doubt its authenticity.

SHARENDEL
Margaret Carr

Ruth didn't want all that money. And she didn't want Aunt Cass to die. But at Sharendel things looked different. She began to wonder if she had a split personality.

MURDER TO BURN
Laurie Mantell

Sergeants Steven Arrow and Lance Brendon, of the New Zealand police force, come upon a woman's body in the water. When the dead woman is identified they begin to realise that they are investigating a complex fraud.

YOU CAN HELP ME
Maisie Birmingham

Whilst running the Citizens' Advice Bureau, Kate Weatherley is attacked with no apparent motive. Then the body of one of her clients is found in her room.

DAGGERS DRAWN
Margaret Carr

Stacey Manston was the kind of girl who could take most things in her stride, but three murders were something different . . .

THE MONTMARTRE MURDERS
Richard Grayson

Inspector Gautier of Sûreté investigates the disappearance of artist Théo, the heir to a fortune.

GRIZZLY TRAIL
Gwen Moffat

Miss Pink, alone in the Rockies, helps in a search for missing hikers, solves two cruel murders and has the most terrifying experience of her life when she meets a grizzly bear!

BLINDMAN'S BLUFF
Margaret Carr

Kate Deverill had considered suicide. It was one way out — and preferable to being murdered.